MATED TO THE CLAN

JADE ALTERS

The air brakes of the bus hissed as the vehicle jolted. My head hit the seat before me, waking me from my travel-fevered sleep.

"Ouch."

"Watch it, lady," groused the passenger ahead of me.

"Oh, for heaven's sake," I muttered. It wasn't my fault the vehicle stopped suddenly.

"What did you say?" said the man. He twisted and squinted at me angrily.

"I said I pray to the good Lord I don't have occasion to use the hunting knife in my backpack." I gave him a sunshiny smile to put on a psycho air, but I also know bus drivers don't play when it comes to disagreements. We could both get booted off. Mr. Angry Man seemed aware of this too, and with a glance to the driver, he grunted and put his eyes forward.

Reflexively, I fingered my mother's locket, something she always wore, and now I wore in memory of her. Her passing two months ago hit me hard. I missed her horribly and the fact that I was running from my past once again did nothing for my mood.

Buses are a long, hard way to get somewhere, but if you travel to the middle of nowhere and have no car of your own, they're a necessary evil. On either side on this two-lane highway is a wall of green that claimed the broken back of the Appalachian Mountains. The right side was mostly one long stretch of tree line that climbed the slopes of a mountain range eaten away by a half billion years of existence. Along the left, the land tumbled steeply into a one of the uncounted long lakes of the region. The only relief was the occasional house, or a reddish-brown farm stand clinging to the side of the highway, as if cutting into the interior represented some great danger. Every minute of the ride stretched out as if the Universe expected you to examine the beginning and end in infinite detail before you could pick up the next moment of time.

That's why my lids grew heavy, and I leaned my head between the crack of the seat and wall of the bus, cushioned by my jacket.

"Hurry, Ainsley, hurry."

"Wha—" I'm half-asleep and my mother is trying to lift me, but I'm a big girl. Daddy said so. "What's wrong, Mommy?"

"We've got to go now."

"Mrs. Lane, we have to hurry."

I stared in the eyes of the big man who stood next to Mommy. His clothes were dark, and he sort of looked like a policeman. The policeman came to school often, and he was nice. This man—I don't like him. Mommy looked scared.

A motorbike rumbled on the street. Daddy's coming home.

"Oh God," Mommy gasped.

"I'll get her. You get to the van."

The big man picked me up, and I kicked and screamed. Daddy was coming home, and I wanted to see him. I was so upset and crying because the man was taking me away from my daddy that I forgot Ginger Bear.

"Ginger Bear! Ginger Bear! I want my bear!" I screamed as the man put me in the black van and climbed in as Mommy snapped on my seatbelt.

"We'll get you another one," she said.

"Go!" called the man. The van lurched forward, and I screamed in my fright.

My head hit the back of the forward seat again but it seemed now I reached my destination.

"Clarkstown!" called the driver.

I gathered my backpack and my jacket, checking twice before I walked away. Since that night, I always checked twice before I left a place. If I lost something, I might not get the chance to retrieve it again.

Much of my life was like that. We moved to more places than I could remember. I didn't understand until I was older that the person we ran from was my father. I didn't know what a bad man he was.

Dangerous.

Criminal.

Wanted.

Road weariness sizzled through my bones as I stepped shakily from the bus. The driver had pulled my luggage, and it sat forlorn on the ground.

"Is that it?" he said.

"Yes."

He looked at me expectantly, and I dug into my pocket for a dollar, the last one I had. There was some money in my online account. But things looked grim in the one-street town, tenanted with one large building whose sign marked it as the General Store, and a single gas station. I may not find an ATM to draw out some cash here.

Maybe it's better that way.

He glanced at the dollar and twisted his mouth in disapproval but screw him. I wasn't flush with cash, and I would not spend it like I was.

"Thanks for a pleasant ride," I said as I picked up the luggage. He grumbled and climbed the stairs to his seat. There wasn't even a rest stop for him and the other passengers before he rolled out leaving me behind.

With a groan of tires on gravel, the bus pulled away, and a man stood at the doorway of the gas station. It wasn't hard to notice him. Apparently, they grow them big here in Maine because this guy was six-one of solid muscle with a jaw square enough to cut glass. His green eyes twinkled from under a baseball cap.

"You must be Ellie."

"I am."

He walked forward and stuck out his hand. I offered mine, and he took it, covering my tiny hand completely, but instead of squeezing it, sheltered it with its warmth. I looked up into his eyes and saw only welcome.

"Cole Clark."

"Nice to meet you, Mr. Clark."

"Cole."

"Ellie Harper."

He smiled slowly and broadly as if he hid a secret. "I thought we established that already."

My eyes narrowed. This guy wasn't poking fun at me, was he? And no, I am not nervous. There's no reason to be even if the most gorgeous guy I've ever seen is holding my hand. Those butterflies fluttering in my stomach are from too much coffee and too little food in the past three days.

"I'll take that," he said, releasing my hand and reaching for my luggage exactly at the same time as my stomach squelched in its underfed state.

"Our next stop is the General Store. You best stock up on

whatever eats you want because I only come into town once a week."

"Um, ah," I said, my face turning red because it suddenly washed over me how ignorant I was about my present surroundings. "Does it take debit cards?"

He smiled amused by my naivete.

"Debit cards?" he asked as if he never heard of them.

Oh shit. What the hell would I do now?

The door of the gas station opened, and a man bigger than Cole in a sheriff's uniform stepped out holding a cup of coffee and walked to us. He was six-two at least, with arms that look liked they'd seen plenty of time in the gym or hauling logs. One never knew in the middle of nowhere in Maine.

"This man bothering you, ma'am?" he said with an air of authority that did not brook disrespect.

"Sheriff," said Cole coolly. "Ms. Harper just asked if the General Store took debit cards."

"And you asked what debit cards are," he said with a rumble of disapproval.

Cole gave a slight shrug of his shoulders.

"So, you *are* bothering her. No wonder the census is down at the lodge if you keep harassing the customers. And you the manager. Apologize to Ms. Harper."

Wow. Law-and-order in Clarkstown extended to enforcing courtesy. This sheriff was a hard-ass.

Instead Cole chuckled.

"Ms. Harper, meet Sheriff Zain Clark, my cousin and co-owner of the Clarkstown Lodge."

"Damn straight," rumbled Zain.

"Nice to meet you, Sheriff."

"Call me, Zain. We *will* share digs."

Sharing? What?

The sheriff's eyes glinted with mischief, and I got that for the second time in two seconds I got played.

"Who's pulling her leg now?" said Cole with exasperation in his voice. "You have your own cabin, Ms. Harper. In fact, I've started up the wood stove already so it will be nice and cozy when we get there. No, Zain, and my other two cousins, Marcus and Drew, live at the main lodge with me. But since guests usually spend most of their time in the lodge, it's easy to think we are living together. But don't worry, Zain has promised not to harass the guests this season."

"Says who?" said Mr. Law-and-Order with a smile.

"Let's go, Ellie, before he cuffs us for his own amusement."

"He does that?"

"He wishes," snorted Cole.

"I'll see you later," said Zain smiling. "Oh, and to answer your question, Ms. Harper, the cashless society follows us even into the depth of Maine's woods. Your debit card works at any of Clarktown's fine establishments."

"Yeah," said Cole. "All three."

ZAIN

It was a busy day, so there was no time to think about the adorable woman that rented a cabin from us. I forgot what Cole said about how long she'd stay. Cole told me she wanted a quiet place to work. Most of our female guests were twenty years older. Now I wish I had listened more because I could see how five foot-seven of blond hair and curves could spice things up.

I purposely ignored that this was precisely what I berated Cole for regularly. He fell in love at least once a summer and built a sizable little black book for hook-ups. Somehow the women never stuck to Cole, they knew he wasn't long-term material. But they would need to leave city life behind and move in with a backwoodsman and his three cousins. So, Cole remained the "summer attraction" for the lodge, a role that we all disparaged and secretly envied.

Well, everyone but me.

No.

Really.

I pulled the cruiser over to the General Store which doubled as the government center of our little town. The post office was there, as well as a single room we shared with the town clerk, Mrs. Ahern, who only kept office hours three days a week. Drew was there, going through the mail.

"Hey," he said brightening when he spotted me. "Have you heard about the bear and the stripper?"

"Probably," I said as I lifted the hinged part of the counter that let me into the desk area. "You've regaled me with every one of your jokes at least five times.

"Then, why did the turtle cross the road?"

I picked up the mail and flipped through it. "Ask Marcus. He's the game warden of the family."

"You're no fun," he complained, and I arched an eyebrow at his remark.

"Okay, here's a new one. A little law enforcement humor."

I sat at my desk and pressed the power button on my computer. "Go ahead," I said, hoping he kept this short. If Drew got the jokes out his system now, my cousin would slow down for the rest of the day.

"Get this. A man breaks into a home in the middle of the night and searches for valuables with a flashlight when he hears a voice say, 'Jesus is watching you.' Startled, the man looks around quickly, but doesn't see anything, so he continues his search. He goes to pick up a stereo when he hears again, 'Jesus is watching you.'

"Now freaking out, the thief scans the room more carefully for the source of the warning and sees a parrot on a perch in the corner. The thief then whispers, 'Was that you?'

"The parrot replies, 'Yes, it was.'

"Amused with the bird, the thief says, 'Thanks for the warning, but I'm an atheist. So, what's your name?' And the parrot answers, 'Moses.'

"Now laughing out loud, the thief asks, 'What kind of people name a parrot Moses?' And the parrot replies, 'The same kind that name their Rottweiler Jesus.'"

"Uh huh," I said.

"What? Not even a little funny?"

"No. Hey, did you pull the recent most-wanted off the FBI site?" I stared at one face, a one percenter biker on the run for drug trafficking, and he seemed familiar. I glanced at the name—Xavier Lane. Nope. Don't know him,, but I sent it to the laser printer so I can stick it on the bulletin board.

"Like one of them will show up here."

"I don't know. It's easy to get lost on the Trail. Marcus told me last night that some hikers complained to him about some suspicious characters hanging out on the Trail."

"Uh, huh," Drew said, unconvinced. "One. It's too damn cold at night right now to sleep up there. Two. Hikers aren't likely to come across hardcore mountain men waiting for someone to find them suspicious."

"That is exactly what I told Marcus. But you can't be too careful."

"Did you see the request from Dunlop County for extra help during their Motorbike Festival?"

I had pushed the request aside. We are a two-man operation for four thousand, though mostly uninhabited, square miles. I didn't like sending one of us off to another county.

"Yes."

"I'd like to go."

"No."

"Things have been quiet here, and to tell you the truth, I'm a little bored."

"In that case—no."

"Alpha asshole," Drew grumbled, turning back to his computer.

The office door swung open, and Marcus entered.

"Hi, Stumpy," Drew greeted, in rare form today. "Did you hear the one—"

Marcus drew the unfortunate nickname of Stumpy since

he went to the SUNY School of Forestry. The denizens of that school tended to suffer that nickname.

"Yes."

"But you didn't even—"

"Yeah, I did. You talk in your sleep. Loudly. Right through the walls."

"I do not," Drew said .

"Suit yourself. But I now know your passwords for your phone and your laptop."

"You do not."

Marcus chuckled. "But now, just to be sure, you'll have to change them anyway."

"Bastard," Drew muttered as he pulled his phone out.

"And this," said Cole loudly, "is the Sheriff's and Town Clerk's office." The office door swung open once more, and I swear every pair of eyes fell on Ellie Harper.

Ellie stared at us as if she'd never seen four men in the same room together.

"Well," said Marcus, "who is this?"

"This is our newest guest, Ellie Harper," said Cole, narrowing his eyes at Marcus. "Ellie, this is our local game warden, Marcus Clark."

"Another Clark man in uniform," she mused.

"At your service."

"I suppose you're another cousin as well?"

"Guilty. Now I see why smoke rose from the chimney of the Moose cottage this morning."

"Moose cottage?" said Ellie. "There's not a moose head hanging on the wall, is there? I couldn't stay in a cottage with a dead thing staring at me."

"Sure there is," said Drew brightly. Cole gave him a cutting glance that would have shut up any smart person.

"We'll make sure," I said, "that we take it down for the duration. It's our nicest cottage, and we wouldn't want you to miss that. Marcus, on your way out to patrol, can you stop by and take the moose head down?"

"Sure, Zain, no problem." He gave Cole a smug smile that said 'Hey, I'm scoring points with the lady.' Cole, standing behind Ellie, bared his teeth.

"Thank you, Marcus," I said. "That would be helpful. Cole, do you need help with the supplies?"

"No. I'm good."

"I'll give you a hand anyway. Drew, print out the new most-wanteds and post them. I'm going to check out Marcus' concern on the trail."

"I'll go with," said Drew. "I've sat in the office too long."

"No. I'm fine. Someone has to man the office while Mrs. Ahern is out. And tell the Sheriff of Dunlop County that you'll go help them out."

"Wait? What's the catch?"

"No catch. We're just showing solidarity for our brothers in law enforcement." I pulled my trooper hat off the hat rack. "Call me if anything happens."

"Yeah," said Marcus. "Let us know about your new high score on Warcraft."

"You wish you could do as well at Warcraft."

"Bye, Drew," I said.

"So," Ellie said as we walked the hallway to the front of the store. "All of you are cousins? And you live together?"

"The lodge," said Cole, "is part of the family trust. Clarks have lived on the land for one hundred and twenty-five years."

"That's impressive. I haven't lived anywhere—well, never mind. The pictures on your website are gorgeous. I can't wait to see it."

"I look forward to showing you around," said Cole.

Damn, Mr. Charm had zeroed in on her already. For reasons beyond my understanding, this time I mind. This is not like me at all. And then, me sending Drew off to the motorcycle rally? Why the hell would I do that?

"Cole, how are the repairs going on the cabins?"

"Fine. We have weeks before Memorial Day."

"Is that when your usual season starts?" asks Ellie.

"Our summer season. We have the hunting season and ski season and keep busy in various parts of the year. The middle of January and February is when we get snowed in, and the cabins need a little TLC after they've been vacant during the winter."

"Yeah," chuckled Marcus. "We have to de-critter them."

"De-critter?"

"Deep woods version of decluttering," said Cole. "Don't worry. Your cabin is cleaned and ready."

We all hauled boxes of groceries to the truck. I couldn't help but watch Ellie - her smile, how her body moved, and the bear inside me rumbled his approval. This was not the right time for my animal self to rouse from his winter hibernation and take notice. I'm the Alpha, the leader of the clan, but I was always calmest during winter hibernation when my beast slept and waited for spring. But Ellie roused him in a way other women hadn't.

I was in big trouble.

MARCUS

"I'm chasing a fawn," I said, "to get her out of Mr. Russo's pasture, and she runs me up one side and down the other. She refused to exit the fence hole she came in."

"So, what did you do?" said Ellie. I'm impressed a city girl is interested in stories of my mundane profession. Most days the most interesting thing I do is move a turtle across the road or write tickets for illegal hunting or fishing.

"Mr. Russo and I made a corral with leftover fencing. Between us and his dog, we urged the fawn out of the pasture."

"And I'm sure old man Russo was very grateful," said Cole sarcastically. Mr. Russo was a known curmudgeon.

"Gee," said Drew, "and no blackberries in season as a reward."

My cousins guffawed, and I shook my head. Last year, a similar thing happened but, in the summer, when Russo's blackberry bushes had fruit, and I plucked a few. I was idiot enough to mention it to my so called "friends" here, and Drew crafted it into a standing joke.

"So, what's your line of work?" I asked Ellie, trying to turn the conversation away from me. In truth, this charming creature with her brown eyes and blonde hair had me captivated, and I wanted Ellie for myself. My cousins felt like third, fourth and fifth wheels.

"Ghostwriter. I write books for other authors."

"You mean celebrities?"

She shook her head.

"Fiction. The publishing industry has evolved so quickly, the modern high-volume author can't put out enough books to satisfy demand, so that's where I come in."

"How?" said Drew.

She broke apart her roll and buttered it, one side then the other, weighing her words.

"An author contracts me to write a book to a certain length on a certain theme. Either she gives me an outline, or I write one and submit it for approval. Then I write the book."

"But your name isn't on the cover?"

"In most cases, no."

"That's not right," said Drew. "Another person takes credit for your work."

"Writing the draft is the first step. The author who buys it will edit for tone and style. Rewrites sometimes take as much work as writing the book. Then they'll send it to an editor for another round of edits. If they're indie publishing it, they contract a cover and pay for marketing and spend time promoting the book. The post-writing process can take as many or more hours than the actual writing. And you still haven't seen a single dime of book sales, except an advance which they probably paid to me. Me? I take my money and move on to my next story."

She bit into the roll and her eyes closed, and she sighed. "Delicious."

"But," Drew persisted, like a dog with a bone. "No one knows it's you who wrote it. Don't you want that?"

Her face turned sad, and I could kick Drew for poking her in places she didn't want to go.

"No. I don't need fame. I enjoy writing, and," her face brightened, "I'm one of the lucky few that can say that I make a living at it. So there." She waved one-half of her roll in the air as if making a point, which she did.

"Here," Drew offered, ladling another helping of stew into her bowl.

"No, thank you. I'm not used to eating so much."

"How's the cabin?" I asked. Zain shot me a glance, but yes, I took Bullwinkle from the wall and stuck it in the equipment shed.

"Oh, but you must have room for dessert," said Cole. "I made an apple cobbler."

I've watched how Cole has been watching Ellie, and I dislike it. He gets plenty of action from the other guests. It's time for him to share the wealth.

"You know what would help," I said. "A nice walk by the lake to walk off dinner. Might make room for dessert."

My cousins gave me hard stares, but I can't help it if they didn't think about a moonlight stroll first.

"That sounds good," she agreed.

Fortunately, it was a warm night, or at least not cold enough to drive us inside. We walked at the water's edge where the shimmering water lapped at the constructed sand beach. An earlier generation of Clarks built it, and the successive ones maintained it by bringing in a dump truck or two of sand each season.

The moon was three-quarters full, but it was high in the sky and didn't block out the Milky Way. Here, miles away from the light pollutions of the city, the purplish ribbon snakes through the velvet curtain of night. Constellations—

the light show of the ages--spread above us in all its majesty. It does a bear shifter's heart good to walk in such glorious, raw nature.

"Wow," said Ellie. "It's gorgeous here."

She stood close enough that I catch the scent of her hair and our arms brushed against each other. My bear urged me to put my arm around her, but I don't know how'll she'll respond.

"What's that dark spot in the middle of the lake?" she asked.

"That's Bear Island."

"Oh, doesn't anyone live there?"

"Oh yeah. Lions and tigers and bears," I said.

She shook her head. "None of you can give a straight answer. It's always a joke with you."

"You got me on the lions and tigers, but I assure you that bears do live there from time to time. Females find the seclusion helpful in raising their cubs until they get old enough to swim to shore."

"Bears swim?"

"Like champs. The cubs take to the water quickly, and the calm waters of the lake are the perfect place for them."

"Obviously, my city life has left me undereducated in the ways of the wild."

"Don't worry. You have a native guide right here."

"Thanks." Our footsteps crunched in the sand, and then she stopped and gazed toward the water.

"This is such a peaceful place. I hope I can stay here a while."

"You're welcome to stay as long as you like."

"That's not what I mean, but I appreciate the thought. Say, your cousin is a good cook."

"Yeah, we tease him about sending him to Paris to culinary school, but he tells us he can't bear the thought of us wasting away into skin and bones."

"How considerate," she said drolly.

"Besides, his girlfriends would miss him too much."

The words fell out of my mouth on their own accord like I didn't have the brain power to stop them.

"Girlfriends, as in more than one?"

But if that was bad, my next words just sealed the coffin of being the worst cousin ever.

"I misspoke. Not girlfriends. Rather friends with extreme benefits."

Oh, holy hell. Can I make it sound any worse? Cole's girlfriends were all lovely ladies, and I'm making him sound like a man whore. The ladies would come to visit him regularly, but it was pretty apparent that aside from sharing some good times, neither he nor they had much in common.

I watched Ellie's emotions tumble on her face, from disappointment to resignation, and I kick my ursine self for poisoning Cole's well.

Shouldn't she know? said a traitorous part of me. With a shock, I realized that these thoughts were coming from my bear, or rather the animal side of me that is in hot competition Ellie's affection.

Quiet you, I muttered as if this part of my dualistic nature was separate and apart from my human self. It's not, but it is a shock when my bear asserts himself, especially after a long, quiet winter.

"Pardon?" said Ellie.

"I shouldn't have said that. About Cole, I mean."

Now I've dug a deeper grave to fall into. Although we lead quiet lives, the bear part of us is promiscuous. As bears are in the wild, we are also, which accounted for our frequent trips to Bangor. So, I had no business calling out Cole's behavior.

"Hey," she said gently. "I'm just here to work in a quiet place where I can blot out distractions. I've got two books to write and close deadlines. I won't have time for much else.

My bear did not like her words and my ursine self seemed to grow and command more of my thoughts than I would wish.

"Are you sure?" I said as I edged closer to her. There was a hairsbreadth between us now; I stood over her and bent my head to gaze into the chocolate depths of her eyes. The thinking part of my brain took a hike in the woods as I leaned and brushed my lips to hers. Her soft, welcoming lips drew me like a bee to nectar, delicious and captivating.

I slid my arms around her waist and pulled her close. Her breasts and hips pressed flush with mine, and the flutter of her heart pounded an urgent rhythm older than time. My tongue swept into her mouth, and hers danced with mine in smoldering desire. My inner bear rumbled his approval.

Mate.

I'm too busy to listen to the import of my bear's word, but I second the emotion to get closer to this woman who has captivated both sides of my nature. Our kiss becomes hungry and demanding, and my hands slid to the delicious globes of her ass, giving them a slight squeeze.

But she pulled away quickly, and I stared at her, aroused and confused about what was happening.

"What's that?"

I shook my head since words seem to have taken a hike along with my thinking brain.

"That sound. Something snapped."

It's my bear that responded to Ellie's alarm, and I turned my head to the direction she pointed, Crinkling my nose, I caught an unfamiliar scent. It's human. I had no idea who was spying on us, and I toyed with going after him or taking Ellie to safety.

Safety first.

"I'll walk you to your cabin," I said.

I can't believe how Cole and Marcus fall over Ellie. Sure. She is gorgeous. Long lashes frame liquid brown eyes set in a heart-shaped face with perfect pink bow lips. Ellie's blonde mid-length hair touched her graceful shoulders, topping a lean and willowy body. And she's smart. A writer. You've got to admire that.

It's difficult to craft stories. I've tried but often lose my focus and motivation. That she writes and earns a living from it shows how determined and disciplined Ellie is. The more I learn about her, the more I like her, but my cousins don't give me an in.

Right now, Marcus is walking with her by the lake. I suppose I'm glad it's not Cole because that shifter scores more often than LeBron James. But Stumpy comes a close second. Our Beta is just like any other bear shifter—never met a lady he didn't like. Of all of us, he follows his true bear nature most closely. That he doesn't have a trail of broken hearts in our neck of the woods is due to our reputation as players. The local ladies smile at us indulgently but send us on our way, looking for less feckless hearts on which to hang their star.

Which was why I asked to go to the Motorbike Festival. In places like that, there were plenty of women who don't mind getting up close and personal for a night or two. Sure, I'd be on the clock but not twenty-four seven. And when Zain told me to go, I thought it was great until I realized he cut me out of the running for Ellie. Sure, bears are competitive about females, but this was the first time I'd seen Zain's beast act this territorial over a woman.

"Who's supposed to be on patrol here?" he demanded. Instantly, all our heads jerked from what we were doing which revolved around cleaning up after dinner.

"What's going on?" rumbled Zain.

Marcus' muscles bunched under his shirt as if he was ready to fight, shift or both. Before he could answer, the lodge landline rang, and Cole picked up the phone.

"There's a trespasser on our land. He was near the lake where Ellie and I walked."

"Is Ellie okay?" asked Zain.

"Yes, I protected her." Marcus glared at Zain for daring to question him.

"Well, who's with her now?" said Zain staring back.

"She locked her door."

"Fine. Drew, you patrol her cabin; you, me and Marcus will check out this intruder."

Marcus huffed a rumble from his chest, but he turned and stripped, and Zain and I did the same. In the background, Cole booked another guest, but Zain would have him stay behind. Someone had to secure the lodge especially if an intruder walked our territory.

We stepped into the night, morphing into our bears, our bodies lengthening and expanding, fur bristled from our skin, and claws grew from our nail beds. In our ursine form, our sharp hearing and olfactory senses became razor sharp and we are faster on four legs than two. If someone trespassed on our property, we'd find him.

Or rather, Zain and Marcus would find them. Those two were fearsome hunters in any shape, man or beast, and they'd sort this out. Me? I'm on guard duty.

But I don't mind. It brings me closer to Ellie, and I'm glad to keep an eye on her.

I paced the perimeter of the cabin snuffling the ground and froze when I picked up an unfamiliar scent. The odor jacks my alert level to high, and I considered calling Zain and Marcus. But I'm more than a match for a single human, and the scent faded anyway. Whoever stood here staring at Ellie's cabin left hours ago.

The light in the cabin flickered and spilled onto the front porch. A few minutes later, a teapot whistled. She must be exhausted, wanting to sleep and yet too keyed up to relax and close her eyes. My bear very much wanted to enter that cabin and reassure her everything would be fine, but that wouldn't work. I barely knew her.

Still, I'm concerned and move closer to the window to make sure she's okay, and that was my mistake. Ellie's glance flicked to the window, and she shrieked.

She must have seen me. Idiot me. I ran to the lodge, shifted then skidded into the great room and gathered my clothes.

Cole poked his head out of the kitchen.

"What's going on?"

"Nothing," I said

"Did Zain and Marcus find anything?"

"No," I said as I pulled taut the ties on my sneakers. I ran out and headed directly to Ellie's cabin, hoping that Zain and Marcus were too far away to reach it before me. Surely, they had heard her scream and would come running.

Breathlessly, I knocked on her door.

"Who is it?" Her sweet voice held a tremor, and the stress in her voice hit home it was me that made her anxious.

"Drew," I said. "I heard you scream."

She cracked open the door revealing a sliver of her body and one brown eye.

"I'm okay. There was a shadow in the window. It went away."

"Perhaps I should come in and look around. You know, check the doors and windows."

I am a duplicitous rat because I can check the windows from the outside of the building. But my bear, that traitor, didn't care what animal it imitated to get closer to delectable Ellie.

"That's right," she said nodding as if to reassure herself. "You're the deputy sheriff. Okay. Look around."

"Sure." I strolled inside and immediately my eyes went to the stone fireplace and the conspicuously empty spot where the moose head usually lived. It didn't seem right Old Moosey didn't hang in his usual spot, but Cole accommodated Ellie. I caught Marcus' faded scent from earlier.

"You didn't sound sure you should let me in," I said, checking the first window on the right and finding it locked.

She shrugged. "Men in uniform don't make me feel safe."

Though I found her response cryptic, I continued to check the windows, going through the small cabin room by room. The rustic shack had four—the living room/kitchen area, two bedrooms, and a bathroom.

I came out of the last to find her staring at me.

"The windows are locked," I said.

"Thanks," she said. "Um, would you like tea?"

"You sure you want me here? Since you said men in uniform don't make you feel safe."

"I'll take a man in uniform over a wild animal?"

"Oh," I said.

"I thought I saw a bear."

"They're all over the place," I said. "The dumpster draws them."

Ellie took the kettle off the stove and poured water into two cups.

"Dumpster?"

"Behind the main lodge. Since it's just us in the winter, we don't get the trash picked up as often. It gets—"

"That's okay. I don't need a graphic description."

"As long as you stay in the cottage you'll be fine."

"That's easy for you to say. I'm not an outdoor girl."

"Yet you came here."

"I'm thinking I made a mistake." She offered me a cup of tea, and I took it as I leaned against the counter.

"I don't think so," I said as I stared into her brown sugar eyes. Her inviting scent practically begged for me to touch her. "I'm glad you're here."

"Yes," she said smiling ruefully. "Everyone has been very welcoming. Except, maybe Zain. He seems distant."

"He likes you fine," I said thinking he stared at her too much. I saw how his nostrils flared at dinner. My cousin wasn't apt to hook up as much as the rest of us, but there was no mistaking how his eyes tracked her every move.

"Marcus," she said, "tells me Cole has a bunch of girl-friends."

I shrugged my shoulders. "I wouldn't say that. They are more like friends with extreme benefits."

"Marcus said the same thing."

"We tease him about it enough. He's our cousin, and we don't cut him slack. So, he dates one or two of the ladies during the summer. We wish we were so lucky."

"You can't get lucky?" she said with a sly smile.

"You tell me," I said. Her eyes open wide as I leaned forward and pressed her lips against mine. The tantalizing taste of her flesh provokes a need for more and I became a man who didn't know he was starving. Cradling the back of her head with my hand, I pulled her closer, lost in desire and the ancient call of my inner beast for his mate. I wasn't thinking about this, just how I could get more of this delicious creature—now.

When I brushed my fingers up her inner thigh, and she made a small noise in her throat, I took it as approval. My fingers traveled between her legs to do the talking, and she squirmed underneath my fingertips. Boldly, because I do not take prisoners, I unzip her tight jeans and dip my fingers inside.

"Is that good?" I whispered.

"Yes," she gasped. "So good."

"You are so beautiful."

"Ummm," she replied as I stroked her. My mouth found hers again, and our tongues met. I am consumed with every touch, and I found her neck especially appealing. There was no thought other than the pure enjoyment of listening to her moans. Her heat flooded my fingertips. She tensed, and her back arched as I quested for the sweet spot between her legs where heaven lives.

"Drew, Drew," she murmured between the sexy little whines that escaped her throat. I found her sweet entrance and curled my fingers inside. She gasped, her cream flooded my hand, and then she collapsed against me. After nibbling her neck, I instinctively bit into her tender skin. My inner bear rumbled his approval as I moved to pick her up and take her into a bedroom when a knock on the door shattered the mood.

COLE

I should have let my cousins ship me to Paris years ago because they all ticked me off. Zain and Marcus left without a word while I booked a new guest and that jerk Drew sniffed around Ellie's cabin. In any other sport, a ref would call this play foul, but the game of love has no rules.

There's no secret that bears compete for females, and it is most definitely my inner bear nature that guided my actions. The first minute I saw Ellie, he woke, sniffed and *wanted* her. And this desire differed greatly from my other dalliances. It was an itch that grew into a persistent vexation. The need to get closer to her overrode my common sense.

Why this woman out of hundreds who wandered through our lodge since my teen years?

It also didn't escape me how my cousins looked at her too, and my bear growled and gnashed his teeth complaining about it. *Not like there aren't other fish in the pond, dude.* I'm not sure whom to direct that thought, my bear or my cousins, but I suspected that I'd soon find out.

That idiot Drew was sniffing around Ellie, and I would

not let that happen. Only while my cousins scoped out the territory, Zain expected me to stay here and watch the lodge. We have some expensive possessions here--the sixty-inch wide screen on the wall, the lodge computer with its ridiculously costly hotel management software to name a couple things. Not that anyone has bothered us, but there's always the first time. But I still hated that I was stuck here in the lodge while the others patrolled and that jerk Drew hung around Ellie's cabin.

These thoughts grew in my mind as I finished sticking the dinner dishes into the dishwasher and put the apple cobbler away. Then I thought, "Why let a fine cobbler go to waste?"

Not that my cobblers ever do, and it would get devoured in the morning for breakfast, but Ellie would miss out and we couldn't have that, could we?

My devious bear made perfect sense to me, even with a trespasser threatening the property. Zain would be unhappy that I left the lodge unguarded while they investigated. Screw that. That bastard Drew was sniffing around Ellie's cabin.

So, with perfect conviction that I'm doing the right thing, I scooped a hunk of the cobbler into a glass storage bowl. This would make it easier for her to warm it in the microwave. And again, I'm aware it's my bear's bidding I'm doing and not my human side when I stopped in front of the mirror by the door. I smoothed my blond hair, courtesy of my mother's genes.

The early May night was chilly, prickling my skin. However, I strode with as much bravado as I could muster across the lawn to the largest and closest cabin to the lodge. Yellow light illuminated the windows which I took as a good sign, but there was no sign of Drew, which was not.

An unhappy growl rumbled in my chest thinking Drew took advantage of proximity to move in on Ellie. Maybe

Drew took a wider perimeter in guarding the cottage, but I don't think so. As I got closer to the door, I caught his scent, and I was *not* happy. Then I looked through the window by the door to see Drew all over her, and that was the last straw.

So, I knocked on the cabin door and waited, my cobbler in hand, and Drew opened the door—no, filled the doorframe, because he's a big guy. We're the same height, but he has more muscle courtesy of the Clark genes he favors. Drew smiled that shit-eating grin of his, and I wanted to wipe it off his face with my fist.

"Hi, Cole," he says brightly. "Aren't you supposed to be watching the Lodge?"

"I didn't want Ellie to miss out on the cobbler. If it doesn't disappear during the night, you guys will scarf it in the morning."

"Thanks," he said, holding out his hand.

"I'd rather give it to her myself," I said. "Excuse me."

Drew frowned and stood his ground which only demanded more forceful methods.

"Hey, Ellie, it's me, Cole. I brought gifts."

Drew growled low in his chest, but I smiled back.

"Hi, Cole. Come in."

Drew moved aside reluctantly, and I entered the cabin. Although I was in it just this morning cleaning it, and this place was as familiar as my own room, it seemed different. It wasn't the missing Moosehead either, which I never liked. It was a relic from my grandfather's time when he or one of his cousins brought the beast down and had it mounted.

No. It was Ellie, standing by the sink. She brightened the entire cabin by her presence, and I moved to her like a moth to a flame.

Her cheeks blushed rosily, and I caught that asshole Drew's scent all over her, and again the thought of fist meeting jaw had a certain appeal. But women never appreciate violence, so I kept a lid on my bear as I offered my gift.

"My cousins will devour this before you get a chance to have some."

"That's very thoughtful, Cole," she said with a shy smile.

"You can warm it in the bowl in the microwave. It's tempered glass."

She put the bowl on the counter.

"Thank you. You all have made me feel welcome. I appreciate it."

"You're always welcome here, Ellie," I said.

I need some alone time with my woman, and Drew just stood there staring at us. Screw that. I would not allow my cousin to cock block me.

"What's that?" I said.

"What?" said Drew.

"That noise. I heard something outside."

"I didn't hear anything," said Drew. Suspicion crept through his voice.

"Still, you should check it out, shouldn't you?"

Drew cast a frustrated dark glance at me, knowing I had trapped him. If he didn't go out and check things out, he'd look like an ass. I beamed angelically at him, and he shook his head. I could practically hear the invectives he muttered to himself.

"Fine," he said.

"And I'll just stay here with her just in case."

"Of course, you will," said Drew. "I'll be back in a few minutes. This shouldn't take long."

"Take all the time you need and do a thorough job. Zain wouldn't be happy otherwise,"

"Fucker," rumbled Drew under his breath. My sharp bear hearing caught it while Ellie turned toward the refrigerator to put the cobbler inside, and Drew left.

"Is everything okay?" she said over her shoulder.

"Of course. Why wouldn't it be?"

"Because the four of you seem on edge. Is there something going on that I don't know about?"

What do I tell her? Right now I don't want her alarmed. Nothing has happened other than we think someone was walking around on the land, but that's not new, though it is a little early for the local youth to sneak into our small lake.

The only thing I'm interested in is getting closer to sweet Ellie, so I moved closer to her.

"Are you sure you don't want me to warm that cobbler for you," I said in a low voice.

She whipped around.

"Cole," Ellie said breathlessly. I scented her arousal, honey to a horny bear, and I locked my gaze with hers. The rise and fall of her breasts was endlessly fascinating, and her mouth was a beacon calling to me.

I slanted my mouth to hers and took her lips in tender kiss.

"Ellie," I said. "You are wonderful."

"Umm, Cole. I mean, damn."

"I know my cousins have made a play for you. I don't blame them. But I'm quite fascinated by you."

"I hear," she said regretfully, "that you have a bunch of 'friends with benefits.'"

"Yeah. That's true. But I'm thinking I should ditch my little black book, or hand it off to one of my cousins. Up to now I haven't found a woman that I feel as connected to as I do you."

"Whoa," she said. "Isn't that a bit too much, too soon?"

"Clark men are like that. We know what we want when we see it. And I've never said that to anyone else either. All my past girlfriends knew we wouldn't last. I've been honest and spoke the score upfront. But this is different. It seems I've waited forever for you, Ellie.

To show her I meant what I said, I kissed her again, deeper this time, pulling her against my heated body. I'm so hard it's nearly painful, and my rational mind is getting ready to take a long hike as I tasted her tongue and nibbled her neck. There was nothing imperfect about this woman, and I'm thrilled when I feel her hardened nipples through her shirt.

I've got to have her.

But at two sharp raps on the door, Ellie tore away from me, her face flushed and her breathing shallow.

"Come in," she said shakily.

Drew bounced into the cabin and then stared at me with his eyes narrowed. He caught the aroma of Ellie's arousal too, and he was not pleased. I kept my attention on Drew, so I didn't notice another man standing in the door.

I heard a warning sub-vocal rumble coming from Drew's chest, but screw him. It's not like Ellie was his. She's mine.

"What is going on around here?"

Zain's familiar and displeased voice filled the cabin, and I turned to see his impressive bulk filling the doorway. Zain keeps a lid on the intimidation most times. He wasn't an a-hole Alpha as some could be. But right now, he's pissed.

"Cole brought me some cobbler," said Ellie.

"Yes, Cole is good at putting hospitality into the hospitality business. And Drew?" He stared pointedly at Drew.

"I checked the locks on her windows."

"Uh, huh. I'm sure Ellie feels very secure now."

"I do appreciate everything," said Ellie.

"No need for thanks. It's our job to make sure our guests are safe from *all* sorts of dangers. So, guys, let's leave and let Ms. Harper get her rest. She's had a long day."

"I'll just stay and keep an eye out," said Drew.

A-hole.

"That's okay, Drew," said Zain. "Marcus and I checked out the area. Whoever was here is long gone."

He gave us both a glance that brooked no nonsense and though my bear was ready to challenge him, my human self pulled back. The reason that Zain was Alpha, and I wasn't, was because he could and did dominate any of us. One day that may change, but not tonight.

"Good night, Ellie," I said. "I'll see you in the morning."

Last night's beef stew was so good I ate too much, but in this I blamed Cole because he was an excellent cook. Part of my weakness though was that home-cooked meals were things of the past, especially since my mother died. I had no room for Cole's dessert, so I saved the apple cobbler for breakfast. Decadent, I suppose, but I can see why the Clark men would chow down on it. It was divine.

All the attention Cole, Marcus, and Drew lavished on me is overwhelming. Have they not seen a woman before? The way they fawned all over me in the same day was flattering and disconcerting at the same time. The Clark men seemed to be a clan of extremes however, because I could not believe the amount of food they put away. I can't imagine putting away that much food and not being as big as a house.

No. Instead they were built like Mac trucks.

Very sexy Mac trucks.

I suffered an embarrassment of riches. Each one was dreamy, and it would be impossible to pick one. Cole was the undisputed "pretty boy." His perfect physique and blond hair sent me over the edge. But Drew's wide, friendly smile sucked me in, too. Marcus was rugged with the largest forearms I'd ever seen. I felt safe in his arms despite how our kiss was interrupted. And I didn't want to pull away but I recognized the danger in nestling in his arms. I do not need entanglements. And Zain. Well, who could not salivate over the standoffish Zain? He just had that air of utter command that was entirely appealing. Zain could tell me to do almost anything, and I'd do it with a wide smile on my face.

But, like I told them, I had two books to write, and I could afford no distractions. To earn enough money to escape far away from the United States meant writing eight to ten hours a day to finish these books to get my money.

The deposits I took only got me this far, so my head totally had to be into writing, not playing with hunky woodsmen, no matter how hot they were.

I decided to go sit on the beach and work. The sun and fresh air would do me good. Hopefully the Clarks wouldn't mind if I used a lodge towel to rest my butt on. Taking one from the bathroom, I headed to the beach.

It's early, and still slightly cool, so I put on a cotton sweater. The rising sun started to dissipate in the morning mist to my right, and the lake straight ahead glimmered with a gentle current and the touch of sunlight on the water. It was a perfect morning. After spreading the towel and getting comfortable, I opened my laptop to get to work.

I glanced at my outline and gathered my thoughts. The first few words either come easy or hard, but once I started rolling I can keep up the pace and put out a decent word count—as long as I don't have distractions.

"Hey."

I recognized the voice— Drew. He strolled toward me dressed in his sheriff's uniform and sunglasses looking very official.

It was damned sexy.

"Hey, Drew. On your way to work?"

"Yeah, someone needs to get in and open the office. Zain stayed out late last night patrolling the property."

"So, you take trespassers seriously."

"Of course, especially when we have such a gorgeous guest to protect."

"Drew Clark," I said in a teasing voice. "I do believe you are flirting with me."

"Guilty. What's my sentence?"

"A kick in the ass," said Marcus. He walked quickly toward us, pulling a wood beach chair behind him. "Here. You shouldn't sit on the sand. Sand fleas."

Drew scoffed. "We don't have sand fleas."

"Water. Sand. Sand fleas. Especially after we have sand dumped on the beach. You never know."

"Are they as evil as they sound?"

"Sounds like someone hasn't spent much time by the water," said Marcus.

"True."

"They're crustaceans but find human blood tasty. They like to come out when it's damp like this, so it's better not to sit on the sand. Their bite is itchy, and the females like to lay eggs in their victims."

"Yuck." The thought of little crabby things sucking my blood ticked my ick meter. "Thanks for the warning and the chair," I said. The chair was welcome, and hopefully it would be comfortable. I rose and positioned it toward the water. Hopefully these guys would leave soon, and I could get to work.

Then Cole arrived.

"I bring gifts. Coffee," he said holding up a travel mug. "And a bacon and egg sandwich."

"I didn't know meals were part of the room."

"They aren't," grunted Drew. "Dude, stop giving away the profits."

"You're just jealous you didn't think of it first," said Cole.

"Jealous of what, you pompous ass?"

"Hey," said Marcus. His eyebrows knit together in concern. "Settle down."

"Who do you think you are, ranger boy?" snapped Drew. "Stay out of this."

"Yeah," said Cole. "Mind your own business."

"It is my business when you make assess of yourselves. What would Zain say?"

"Zain can kiss my ass," said Cole.

"Kick your ass, you mean," said Drew.

"Cuz, make tracks. Don't you have a cobbler to bake?"

"You should be so lucky," snapped Cole. "You'll be fortunate to get bread and water today."

"You don't have to worry about me. I'll find my own food."

"Sure, that's a better joke than the ones you spit out every day."

"Hey, guys," protested Marcus

"Do you know what's a joke?" spit Drew. "That you think you do anything that's important around here."

"Hey!" protested Cole.

"Any one of us can run this lodge, and you know it."

"But you don't."

"That's right. We bring in the money."

"Hey, the lodge earns too."

"It always did earn. It has nothing to do with you."

"Guys," said Marcus in a warning voice. "Cool it."

"Shut up," both Drew and Cole said.

Marcus stepped in between the two of them.

"No, really. Cool it. Zain would hand both your asses to you acting like this, especially in front of a guest."

"Make me," said Drew.

"Don't test me," said Marcus.

"I think I will."

With a great roundhouse swing, he connected with Marcus' jaw, but the bear of a man just stood there shocked and rubbed his jaw. He glared at Drew.

"Is that all you got?" he said.

"Naw, I've got a little more." With that he jumped Marcus, and both of them rolled in the sand trying to get shots off on each other. But Drew realized he was in trouble because he clung to Marcus even as the bigger man tried to pull away. They both bashed into the chair, skidding the heavy thing in the sand, and I got the idea that these guys were out for blood. My heart pounded watching them scuffle, stunned I was the cause of this fight between cousins.

Ping. Ping. Ping.

"What's that?"

"The gang is shooting at us," said the man in the black jacket. "Bastard. Doesn't he realize his daughter is in here."

"Oh, he realizes, officer. Why do I think I called you? He told me he'd kill both of us if I tried to leave."

My daddy would kill me because mommy took me away? Daddy wouldn't do that, would he?

More gunshots hit the moving van, and then I knew. Daddy would.

The van swerved on the road tossing me from one side of the car seat to the other.

"Gun it," said the man in the black jacket.

The wheels squealed while the man in the jacket yanked the handset of the CB microphone.

"Agents under fire. Transporting witness and one child. Need back up immediately."

Rivulets of tears flowed down my cheek as this childhood memory impinged on the present. I can't help this, the PTSD

I have from that night and years of running, and now there are three men in combat near me. I can't take this.

I stood, looking over the field of battle for a way off the narrow beach. But these guys were everywhere. Drew and Marcus are still rolling in the sand, and Cole tries to pull one off, as he's flung backward to land in the sand.

Never mind sand fleas. These guys were more dangerous.

"Stop!" I cried out. "Stop! This is stupid."

But my cries went unheeded as Marcus and Drew duel. Cole stood and moved toward the line between the grass and sand. There were two men trying to kill each other on the beach, and with one at the head, and the water at my back, there was no escape. I clutched my laptop to my chest knowing I had to make a break for it, but I didn't see how.

Then Zain rushed onto the beach, and he looked as pissed at hell. He practically roared as he stood there.

"What the hell is going on!"

I shrieked and ran as fast as I could to my cabin.

ZAIN

I cannot sleep. After roaming the property half the night looking for the trespasser, I still had a feeling a stranger watched us. My bear sense was rarely wrong, so I listened to it.

It wasn't just the need to keep trespassers off our land. We must keep our secret. The gossip about our family in Clarkstown had silenced since the family meeting hall burned, and our parents died twenty years ago. We would have been dead too, had we not played hooky. The minister who took us so the state wouldn't separate us quelled further whispers about us. He knew the truth but wasn't afraid of what we were.

We are all that's left of the Clark clan. I cannot let any calamities happen. I'm the Alpha, and it's my job to protect us.

Dawn poked sunlight through my window, and I threw off my quilt and paced my room before I realized I could wake my cousins. We all had separate rooms on the top floor of the lodge, but we all had very good ears, and when one of us moved, we were all aware.

With a resigned sigh. I went to the kitchen, opened the

refrigerator door and spotted the cobbler sitting on the shelf in the glass casserole under plastic wrap. My bear has a ferocious sweet tooth, and I couldn't resist. We give Cole a lot of grief for being "the domestic one," but he is a good cook. Plus, he drizzled the one thing that bears cannot say "no" to, honey, on the top, and it called to me. Being the youngest, he spent the most time with Reverend Tracy, and that man, being an incorrigible bachelor, was very self-sufficient. Cole sopped up those life skills.

But a satisfied belly did not calm the feeling that all was not well on our land. While scraping the last of the cobbler off the plate with my fork, I peered out the back window toward the ridge of mountain that bounded our eastern flank. And that's when I saw gray smoke rising through the trees.

I know every inch of our land, where all the guest cabins sat, including the hunting shacks with the barest of amenities, and that's where I saw the smoke. That particular shack sat off an old logging road that we kept graded to get access to that part of the mountain. At this time of year after the running snow melted, that road would be a mass of ruts and gravel, barely fit for any vehicle. Who the hell could get up there? I decided to find out.

Tossing off my terrycloth robe, grabbing my phone and tossing it into a backpack with an "emergency" set of sweats, I walked out on the back porch and shifted. Bears can run twenty-five miles an hour and normal humans about a third of that, eight. The hunting cabin was about five miles away, so I arrived in five minutes as opposed to forty-five.

And time was of the essence.

There was a reason why we had "no trespassing" signs and marked-up tree trunks with Maine's universal sign for that—purple paint all over the place. Fires spread quickly, and the last thing we need is any portion of our land ablaze with a carelessly set fire. Any person lawless enough to trespass wouldn't care about fire safety.

My paws sopped up the dew as I tore across the sodden green meadow that stretched to the foothills of the mountain soaring on the eastern edge of our property. Our property extended to that ridge and two more beyond that. The valleys between the ridges were untamed forest, and we do not advise guests to go there.

Any other day I would enjoy this run, the sunlight shimmering off wet grass while the scent and sight of small animals roused my hunting instincts. But not today - I had something else to hunt.

Rising ground and the early morning dark of the tree line signaled the change of terrain. I dove into the thick underbrush and crashed my way up the slope.

Past my first steps, the treetops obscured the slanted rays of the sun, and my dinner plate-sized paws crushed the brittle leaves of last fall underfoot. It was easier traveling this stretch, and even the fallen trunks of trees that did not survive the winter, were no match for my ursine form.

The forest floor was damp still from recent rains. The push up the mountain included a couple slides backwards in the muddy humus, but I used claws and grit to face gravity and the steep terrain.

The scent of smoke grew stronger the closer I got to the hunting shack. It had the faint aroma of a controlled blaze which reassured me but brought home that an invader dared to step foot on my land.

Cigarette fumes twisted with the smoke and crackle of an open blaze, and my anger burned. Marcus was fond of saying that cigarettes were the number one cause of forest fires. We'd seen our share, especially last December during a long drought and all of us Clarks went to help put out the brush fires that sprang up.

Though our arcadian forests filled with hard woods were wetter than the combustible forests of the western United States, fire was still a danger. The year 1947 still blazed in the memory of many older Mainers as the year that Maine burned. In the last two weeks of October, two hundred fires burned a quarter million acres of forest and wiped out nine towns.

Do I know this person will start a fire? No. But I know he trespassed. And if I find that he's broken into the hunting shack, which is secured with a combination lock, then I'll arrest him for aggravated trespass.

I'm the sheriff. I can do that.

At the edge of the clearing, I spotted him standing by the fire ring outside the cabin. His back is to me, and all I saw was a tall, skinny frame and a hunk of long gray hair tied back in a pony tail. He wore thick boots, blue jeans and a leather jacket with a patch.

A biker.

With a three-rocker patch.

Most bikers are good citizens. Social clubs are fine. They just like to hang out and ride. Those with a single patch, or sometimes a patch and a bottom rocker, are social clubs. But the ones with two rockers and a patch just announce their criminal status.

Now I was on high alert, because these guys don't travel alone. But I sniffed the air and didn't pick up the scent of another human. I shifted, slipped off the backpack, and slipped on the sneakers, sweats and hoodie. It's not as official as my uniform but I'm bigger than this guy, so I'm not worried. I stepped out of the woods.

"Heya," I said in my most friendly Mainer voice.

The guy froze but kept his face away from me.

"I suggest," I said, "that you move along. These are private lands."

"I'll do that," the man said. "When I'm ready."

He turned and faced me. In a second of surreal silence our eyes met, and the face connected with what I read on the internet yesterday.

Xavier Lane. From the FBI's most wanted list.

"Police officer," I called. "Hit the ground and put your hands behind your head!"

Lane dropped his cigarette and ran to the other side of the cabin where I could only assume he left his bike. I charged forward but stopped at the cabin's edge and flattened my back against its outside in case he had a weapon. The click and rough rumble of a motor bike engine turning over greeted my ears, and I rushed forward, determined to yank him off that damned thing.

But I fell face forward, hard enough into leaves to steal my breath. The bastard had stuck a log out perpendicular to the cabin wall. Pebbles flew from his back wheel as he gunned the engine to flee to the logging road, and I had to cover my face with my arms to avoid the stinging projectiles from hitting my face.

But the odor of his bike's motor oil did not mask more smoke coming from the front of the cabin. Cursing I went back to the fire and found his discarded cigarette had lit a small blaze. I kicked out the embryonic forest fire and then the campfire too. I'm thoroughly pissed because by the time I can return to the lodge and get a call out over the radio, the bastard would be long gone.

At least he didn't break the lock. We built the door frames sturdy with oak, and combo locks are a bitch to break open. I unlocked it to inspect the cabin. He had pried open one of the small windows and slid his skinny ass inside. On the floor sat a sleeping bag and backpack.

Thoroughly pissed, I walked back to my backpack, and got my phone to take a bunch of pictures inside and out for evidence. Not that a criminal trespass charge would phase this guy, but I could put out a local arrest warrant for him which would alert other Maine Law Enforcement the guy was in the area. Then I grabbed his stuff and hoofed it back to the lodge, thoroughly displeased with this turn of events.

But the events of the morning didn't tick me off more than seeing Marcus, Drew and Cole in a fight on the beach, that thoroughly frightened Ellie. She was backing away toward the water, clutching her laptop, while appealing for them to stop. But the idiots weren't listening.

So, I charge.

"What the hell is going on here?"

Zain skidded to a stop and glowered at all of us. "Don't you have other things to do than bother our guest?"

Ellie shrieked and ran right by us, and I tried to run after her, but Zain grabbed my arm and jerked me backwards.

"Where the hell are you going?" he growled. Our eyes met and his jaw tightened, and he was ready to beat my ass.

But I'm feeling the same way about him. I did not lower my eyes, and I would not.

"Who the fuck are you," I said, "to talk to us like that?"

Zain held his iron grip on my arm as his disapproval deepened.

"Pardon me?" he said with deadly calm.

"No, pardon me, *Alpha*," I said in my most sarcastic voice.

It would be within his rights to cuff me and send me sprawling into the sand. We'd seen similar behavior from Zain's father toward upstart male clan members and learned that this casual violence was the way of things among our kind. But Zain, raised by the compassionate hand of Reverend Clancey, took a smarter route.

"What the fuck is wrong with you—all of you?" Zain swung his head to meet Cole and Drew's eyes. "Ellie is a guest, a paying customer, and all of you are harassing her like teenage boys who just found out what sex is. Now get about your business and stop bothering her."

Cole grumbled under his breath about just bringing her a sandwich, but Zain rumbled a thoroughly dangerous bear growl, and Cole held up his hands in submission.

"I'll go make breakfast," he said.

"That's the best idea you've had this morning," groused Zain.

Drew brushed the sand off his uniform and inspected it as if trying to decide if it would pass muster. "I'll go open the office."

"You will but hold up. I've got something to discuss with both of you."

Zain's professional law enforcement demeanor snapped into place.

"What's up?" I asked.

"I found Xavier Lane, one of the FBI's most wanted up in cabin eight."

"Where is he?"

"Don't know. He drove off before I could arrest him."

I spotted broken bits of dried leaves on his clothes telling more of the tale than Zain spilled. My cousin had a scuffle of his own which he obviously lost. But he wouldn't admit that and right now I won't make him.

"His description on his wanted posted listing is accurate--5-10, 180 pounds, long gray hair which he pulls back in pony tail, wearing biker leathers, a jacket with a Satan's Son patch."

Zain rattled off his professional description, centering all of us on our jobs. Knowing this guy is around, I'll make extra patrols of the parks. A one percenter on the run will try to keep a low profile on public lands, and even though we were close enough to Canada's border to make a good run for it, the Federal government's ICE efforts and increased efforts by Canada RCMP have made that a more iffy proposition than in the past. He's probably hanging around waiting for some contact to smuggle him over the border or perhaps spearhead a new smuggling operation, a growing lucrative trade for criminal enterprises looking for a quick and fat buck.

"We'll set up rolling patrols for nighttime, each of us taking an eight-hour shift. This guy can be hanging around for any number of reasons, but we want to head this guy to jail."

"Got it," said Drew. Sand still clung to his hair, but he put on his best cop face for Zain's benefit.

"I'll fill Cole in on what's happening and make the FBI report."

"Sure thing," I said, and Drew nodded.

"And don't bother Ellie."

Without another word, Zain turned and marched toward the lodge.

"He can't keep me away from Ellie," muttered Drew.

"Dude, take a number."

"Behind you?"

"Damn straight."

"Stay away from her."

I scoffed. Spotting the wrapped sandwich, I retrieved it.

"You'll have to do better than that," I said.

"Where are you going?"

"Why do you care? You have an office to open."

Drew gave me a sour expression. "You're not—"

"Bye, Drew. Have a great day. And you might want to get the sand out of your hair."

I walked past him with a smile as he ran his hands through his hair, dislodging sand while scoffing. But I tossed him the sandwich, and he caught it in one swoop of his hands.

"Here's your breakfast. Best be going. Zain is not in good mood, and you do have to work with him all day."

"Captain Obvious, aren't you?"

"Nope. Just your friendly conservation officer."

"Bye, Stumpy." I nearly wanted to take Drew out for his snide tone, and I should. But if we had another scuffle, I'd have to change my uniform, and I might not be caught up on my laundry.

We were too old to act like teenagers, and I didn't know what was wrong with us. It's not like we haven't tried to edge each other out competing for female attention before Ellie. But this seemed more serious.

I was scratching my head while I headed to the kitchen and picked up my lunch. Damn it, Cole does so much for us, like making our lunches, that I feel like an idiot for treating him like crap.

Scrambled eggs, bacon and toast sit in casserole dishes on the counter, and I put together my own bacon and egg sandwich. Neither Cole or Zain looked at me, which I suppose I deserve. It's frostier in that kitchen than the ancient freezer walk-in grandpa installed in the kitchen decades ago. Filling my thermos with coffee, I grabbed my lunch bag and headed out the door.

Walking to my truck, my eyes travel to Ellie's cabin, and I thought she might be frightened out of her wits. If Zain wouldn't talk to her, I guess I will.

I knocked and waited.

And waited.

Another knock failed to bring her to the door.

"Ellie, it's Marcus. Let me in."

Slowly the door opened a crack and her brown eyes as soft as a doe's peered at me.

"I'm busy, Marcus."

"I just wanted to apologize for this morning."

"Good. You apologized. Now leave."

"Please don't be like that."

"Like what? Wondering what the hell I got myself in to?"

Oh hell. Did that mean she's considering leaving us. No. She can't.

"We're not like this at all."

"Fine. Really. I have to go."

"Please don't leave."

She laughed harshly.

"I wish I could. But I spent all but my last couple hundred dollars getting here."

I held in my sigh of relief.

"So, I have to finish at least one book before I can leave. Excuse me, I have to get back to work."

Ellie slammed the door hard enough I jumped back. Damn, that woman was angry. And I didn't blame her. I was going to have to do something to get into her good graces.

It seemed my feet, or rather my bear, had a plan to do that right away because of instead of climbing into my truck to start my day, I stood on Ellie's porch, knocking on her door again. I shouldn't have done it, but I did, and I seemed unable to turn away.

"Who is it?"

"Marcus."

"I told you to go away."

"Ellie, please open the door."

"No."

"Please, I want to apologize. Properly."

The door cracked open again.

"What can you possibly say?"

I sucked in my breath. "That you are a breath of fresh air around here."

"Dude, have you not noticed that you live in the backwoods? All you have is fresh air."

"I meant." I stop speaking because gazing at her tongue-tied me, and my thoughts go zero to sixty about kissing those sexy lips of hers. And I knew I wasn't doing myself any favors by not keeping my mouth shut.

"Yes," she said in challenge. "You meant what?"

"I meant that…I'm apologizing for my cousins' and my behavior. We all like you."

"That's obvious."

"And we sincerely didn't mean to frighten you."

"You're speaking for the group now?"

"They'd all say the same thing. We grew up together in the same house after our parents died."

Her eye went wide with surprise.

"All your parents?"

"Yes. It was a tragic accident. Reverend Clancey took us in. So, you see, we're more like brothers than cousins, and the sibling rivalry runs a little deep."

"You are not making me feel any better."

"Look, you have every right to be upset with us, but I'd like to make it up to you if I can."

"I don't know. Like I said, I have a lot of work to do."

"That's okay. You'll have to put your keyboard away sometime, and when you do, I'll be around. I live here, you know."

"Yeah. I kind of noticed."

"So, I'm going to go to work now. But I'd like to do one thing if you'll just let me in a minute."

"What? Will you inspect the window locks?"

"What?"

"That's what Drew did last night."

My bear growled thinking about Drew being that close to her but I was just inches from getting her to open the door, so bear power was not what I needed.

"Then I'm sure he did an excellent job. But I would like to do a critter check."

"A critter check?" she said skeptically.

"Yes," I said with a smile. "Varmints show up all the time."

"Yes," she said. "I'm beginning to see that."

Slowly she opened the door, and I stepped inside.

"Yep," I said. "I sense one varmint right now."

"You do now?"

"Yes," I said shutting the door partway. "And I'm afraid it's me."

With that, I leaned in and kissed her sweet lips, and my bear wanted more than that, but it wasn't in the cards. I smelled that bastard Drew approaching the cabin, and I had to get out of here now just so I didn't tick Zain off by pounding Drew into the ground.

DREW

It was difficult leaving Ellie behind to go to work. Just knowing there was a dangerous criminal hanging around our property made me want to stay and see to her safety. Now that I've recognized her as my mate, there was nothing that I would not do to protect her.

The mate thing is a little tricky for bear shifters. A normal bear doesn't hang around to protect females or help raise cubs. Females often have to protect their offspring from aggressive males. But we are a mix of both bear and human; somewhere in that quixotic mingling comes a bear shifter's propensity to recognize our life mates. It was mysterious, and not all shifters found theirs, but I knew in the deepest part of me that Ellie is mine.

So, as I walked the path to Ellie's cabin and smelled that bastard Marcus. He couldn't be closer than a brother but I was ready to tear him apart for sniffing around my mate.

He bounced down the stairs with a big smile on his face that I wanted to wipe off with a swipe of my bear paw, but I couldn't shift so close to Ellie's cabin. She didn't know what we were, and THAT would be another tempest when I tell her.

"Drew? I thought you were heading to the office."

"And you on patrol."

"I wanted to make sure no critters were bothering, Ellie."

"Seems they are, aren't they?"

"Depends on what you call a critter or a varmint."

"Did you see any varmints?"

Before I could answer, Ellie's scream ripped through the woods behind the cabin. We glanced at each other and then took off running.

I reached Ellie first, sitting in the leaves and rubbing her ankle.

"What happened?" I said.

"What the fuck," sputtered Ellie. Her face was red, and tears formed at the corner of her eyes. "Go to the North-woods, I told myself. It's quiet there. No one will bother you there. Boy, was I wrong!"

Marcus skidded to a stop beside me.

"Are you okay?" he said with genuine concern.

"I thought I saw something, like the glint of a mirror. I came out to look and I heard someone talking. So, I went closer. I couldn't see him because he was behind a tree, but he saw me. He called my name, and I started running."

"Ellie," I said. "You should have called us. We would have taken care of this."

"You two were too busy measuring yourselves," she said derisively.

Dear Lord, she was right. Instead of looking out for her, we were battling each other. It was stupid.

"Did you hurt your ankle?" I said. "Do you think you can stand?"

She shook her head fiercely. "I twisted it good when I fell."

I examined her ankle which was swelling. It didn't seem broken but that didn't rule out hairline fractures.

"Let's take her to the lodge," said Marcus.

I didn't like this, because Cole was there, but someone needed to keep an eye on her. Both Marcus and I had to get to work.

"Fireman's carry," I said, and Marcus nodded his head. She's tiny, can't weigh more a hundred or so, but I could see we'd stand there arguing over who would carry her, so I opted for diplomacy.

Ellie winced as we helped her stand on her good foot, and she swung an arm around each of our necks. In three minutes, we had her at the lodge. Cole ran to make an ice pack, and Zain started grilling her on what she saw. Marcus went to find pillows to put under her foot while I examined it. After asking her to move her toes, I determined she didn't need a hospital visit for them to diagnose what I did—a wrenched ankle.

"Take care of her. We'll go check out the intruder," said Zain to Cole. Our Alpha waved me and Marcus out on the porch. "Show me where you found her and see what we can find. If it's that same guy at the cabin, then we definitely have to find him and bring him in."

"And if it isn't?" I said. I did not like the idea of leaving Ellie here with Cole if there was a criminal running loose on our lands. Not that Cole couldn't protect her, but I was the one who should.

"Then we'll take turns patrolling throughout the day. You are due a personal day."

It made me feel a little better that Zain considered letting me do the day patrol. Marcus gave me a sideways glance, but I ignored him.

"Let's go. Show me," Zain said, all business.

We reached where Ellie fell quickly, and Zain sniffed the area thoroughly.

He turned to us and shook his head.

"I don't get a scent like that one at the cabin," said Zain. Frustration edged his voice.

"So," said Marcus, master of the obvious, "there is more than one intruder on our land."

"We can't be sure," said Zain. He rubbed the back of his neck and paced the area again.

"Maybe you should shift," I said, "and make use of that bearish nose of yours."

Zain scowled, and I knew the feeling. Our bears aren't much larger than our humans selves, but the proportions are different, and he'd have to strip. We aren't shy, having seen it all before and with Ellie laid up in the lodge, no one would see the transformation. But no one wants to stand in their birthday suit in the woods on a frosty May morning. Plus, the process can be painful though that has eased up as we grew older.

"If not for Ellie," he grumbled. Zain pulled at his belt buckle and toed off his shoes, then pulled off his uniform and underwear. We turned our heads out of habit. We've done this hundreds of times and don't need to watch as a two-legged man becomes a four-legged bear. Zain always starts with his face, the nose and jaw becoming his muzzle, as his hair thickens, hands and feet becomes paws, the shoulders narrow, and the waist thickens. Zain was the first of us to master this, and he did it with bear emerging from man in a smooth progression from head to toe.

Our Alpha grunted, and we turned to watch him examine the area, nose to ground, and a certain tree trunk. He sprinted north toward the logging road.

With presence of mind, I picked up his clothes, handed

Marcus Zain's boots, and balled the rest under my arm. We ran after Zain, though we lagged, our heavy boots the only thing giving us traction through the humus and leaves. I lost track of him but following a straight line, we emerged on the logging road where he stood, pacing, tossing his head, grunting and looking thoroughly annoyed. He shook his head and shifted.

"It's not the same man," he announced as I handed him his clothes. "And he didn't meet with the other one on this road."

Marcus handed him his boots. "I'll check on the access gate. If there were two people up here, someone must have cut the chain."

"You do that," said Zain.

"That's not going to stop people from walking around the gate," I pointed out.

"No, but it makes it more difficult to get up on this road without hoofing it a long while," said Marcus.

"We've talked about this," said Zain. "And taken every precaution, from painting everything we could purple, to hanging signs and securing the gate. But an area this size, you can't stop people from trespassing."

We all knew this and usually were very tolerant. While we didn't put up with people camping without paying, we don't mind the occasional stroll in the woods. We have a thousand acres, most of it rough terrain, so patrolling it on regular basis is not feasible with only four of us. If our clan was larger, like in the old days, because with more of us there was more to hide, we'd have regular patrols of the land.

"What worries me," continued Zain, "is the last intrusion most definitely centered on Ellie. And we didn't have this number of problems until she got here."

"You can't think she's involved with these men?" I said. My bear highly protested that Ellie would be involved with anything criminal.

"Maybe there's more to her than we know. We need to check her out."

"By 'we' you mean you," I said.

"Yes. A criminal element may be following her, and where criminals run, law enforcement follows. We do not need the potential exposure of our secret an investigator can bring. So, Marcus, you get to work and do a good surveil of the area. Drew, you patrol our land, and I'll get into the office and see what I can find on Ellie Harper."

COLE

llie sat on the couch in the large lodge common room pecking at her laptop that I had retrieved for her. Her foot was propped on pillows and wrapped in towels and ice. She looked helpless, and this alone roused my bear and his protective instincts. Every two minutes I peered into the common room to check on her.

Our kisses have inflamed my desire for her to an outrageous level. I had to relieve my lust twice with my hand before I could sleep. Being in the same building with her sent me up the wall. I needed her, but we weren't there yet. If things continued like they were, it just might scare Ellie off, and I could allow that to happen.

Because I was preoccupied, I forgo that we have a new guest checking in at 11:00 AM, and I needed to prepare his cabin.

"Ellie," I said. "I have to fix up a cabin for a guest. I'm going to lock the doors. If someone knocks, don't worry about it. I'll see them from where I am and come answer it. Do you need anything before I leave?"

"No. I've got my water, snacks, phone, computer and

these lovely crutches you hunted up. I'm good. A little quiet will help me concentrate."

"I haven't disturbed you, have I?"

She bit her lip, which drove me insane, because it was sexy as hell, but she shook her head.

"A girl can't complain about a man waiting on her hand and foot, but I do need some quiet time to make some word count."

"Your wish, mi'lady, is my command. Quiet time coming right up. But if you need anything, install the Clarkstown App on your phone, and enter your cabin number. There is a call button there, so use it if you need me."

Even with these precautions, I made up the cabin quickly, because I was uneasy about leaving Ellie alone. And I changed the cabin too, from being next to Ellie's to the second one over. It was an impulsive move, rationalized by the idea that it was a nicer cabin, and there was no reason not to give the man an upgrade, but the truth of it was, I didn't like the idea of any male closer to Ellie than necessary. I had no idea if Mr. Ortez was young, old, buff or wore a beer gut, but it made no difference. My bear staked a claim on Ellie, which would cause problems with Zain because he wanted us to leave her alone.

I was not a believer of the whole "true mate" thing, but then again, being the youngest of the four of us, I didn't notice my parents or any of the others in their mate bonds. Sure, Mom and Dad loved each other, but I was too young to understand the depths of that. Maybe I still was.

Except when I see Ellie, my breath catches in my throat, and my heart beats faster, and my dick stirs, and I *want* her. And not just for a night, or for now, but for always.

And that's a thought that shattered my brain. The guys give me grief for the women I've hooked up with, but the truth is, as a bear shifter it seemed I lived the promiscuous propensity of my bestial nature more than the others. The ladies didn't mind. Most of them were looking for a little fun, and that's what we had. But no one declared their love for me, and why would they? From the outside, I was a perfectly content hotel manager without any prospects for more than that. We weren't particularly rich, and the Maine winters are legend in their brutality. I was not a catch and didn't mind that I wasn't.

Until now.

I spot from the bedroom window of cabin number three a non-descript older model car pulling into the parking area. This must be the new guest taking an early vacation. At least that's what Mr. Cortez told me. But he didn't seem like the typical oldster looking to get in some spring fishing. And he only pulled from his vehicle a single bag and no fishing gear. He was maybe in his late twenties, five foot eleven, lean and wiry, so about one eighty-five? Zain and Drew were better at gauging height and weight, as that was part of their jobs.

He walked toward the lodge, bag in hand, and immediately my skin prickled and the hair on the back of my head stood at attention. He was walking toward Ellie, and I couldn't have that.

I told myself that this was ridiculous. This man was no threat to Ellie or us, but I rushed out of the cabin anyway.

"Hey!" I said with a friendly wave of my hand. "You must be Mr. Cortez."

"Orlando," he said, holding out his hand which I shook it briefly.

"Sure." I reached for his bag. "I'm Cole Clark, manager of Clarkstown Lodge."

"You're the guy I spoke with last night."

"That's right. If you follow me, I just got your cabin ready for you. Well, mostly ready. I just lit the pellet stove, so it's a little chilly yet."

"Don't I have to check in?"

"Naw. Our census is light right now. Easy enough to keep track of who is here."

"Is there anyone else?"

I didn't like how he said this. Like he was probing for information.

"It's off season. There's me and my three cousins. We've one guest. She needs quiet time for her work. Keeps to herself."

"I see."

My feet clattered up the stairs to the porch of the cabin. "Say, what made you choose us? Our usual clientele are regulars that come here every year."

"I guess I needed a little quiet time myself," he said.

That wasn't much of an answer, and my bear woke up and checked this guy out. Even though his credit card and ID ran through fine, I got the sense he was not telling me the entire story.

Now I had another thing to worry about because I didn't know why this guy was here, and my bear didn't trust his story.

I opened the door and waved him in. Cortez stood just inside the door, taking in the rustic homeyness of the log cabin. The logs were squared so the walls were flat, and elastic sealant used for chinking nowadays kept the cabin relatively air tight. The pellet stove in the center of room venting out the old stony chimney had done its job and warmed up the cabin.

The furniture were various pieces made by Clark men over the decades, some attractive, and some not so. There was a kitchen table and chairs, a wicker couch with pads made from stuffed quilts made by various Clark women, a wicker chair and smaller tables.

Some Clark men, however, were not talented in woodworking, and some of the worst pieces we had I've long since "recycled" for the Hammer mill that pulverized them to dust so I could make pellets. Making our own pellets takes a little time but was worth it monetarily. Using the biomass from around the lodge was a cost-effective way to heat cabins and gave me some alone time from my cousins.

"It looks fine," said Cortez.

"There is a microwave in the kitchen and a propane stove for serious cooking, and the refrigerator. Sorry, no dishwasher. The water is well water, so don't worry about using too much cold water. Take it easy on the hot water though. It's a small tank."

"That's fine."

"You did remember to bring in your own food? That's not part of the accommodations."

"Well, I thought I'd pick up stuff here."

"We don't open our lodge store until Memorial Day. But there's a general store in town. That's the closest. Otherwise you'll have to drive a ways to the next town to find a grocery."

"I guess I better go shopping."

"Here's your key. If you need anything, come up to the lodge, or use our app."

"You have an app?" His voice was skeptical and impressed at the same time.

"Yeah. Drew, my geeky cousin made it. Comes in handy. It's free on the app store. Just look for Clarkstown Lodge."

"I'll do that."

"Towels, soap and shampoo are in the bathroom."

"How about that? A five-star cabin in the woods."

"A little more than that. When you look out the window tonight, you'll see a million billion stars."

"I'm looking forward to that."

"We have a small beach, but the water's too cold for

swimming. We usually rent canoes, but they are in storage right now. If you need one, let me know and I'll pull one out."

"No, I'll content myself with walks."

"That's fine. We've got seven square miles of area you can wander through, though you might want to inform the desk if you go out farther than the top of the ridge. We wouldn't want you to get lost and then send out Marcus to fetch you. He's our local conservation officer, and he'll find you but give you a stern lecture about hiking safety.

"I'll keep that in mind," said Cortez with a smile.

"Good. Then I'll get on to my other work. Nice to meet you, Orlando."

"Bye."

I walked away, but I did not like this man on our property. And when I turned at the door to say a final goodbye, I caught a glint of metal under his jacket as he bent to pick up a magazine. From Zain and Drew, I knew very well what this was.

A gun.

What the hell was our guest doing with a gun?

I had to tell Zain and as quickly as possible.

If my head wasn't swirling with the attention of the Clark cousins, all of this would be meaty material for a romance novel. Three hot guys after me? Oh man. Never in my life did I have this problem. Heck, I didn't even have a high school boyfriend because of how many times we moved.

I grew up in Witsec, government protection, and they shuttled us from one place to another quite a bit. My father, it seemed, had tendrils everywhere. If it wasn't his club, Satan's Sons, tracking us down, a one-percenter club looked to cash in on the bounty that my father posted. Mom knew better than to hang out in the biker bars but since the advent of the digital age, it was easy enough to send a text with a picture. Mom was terrified of going out, and I only did because I had to go to school. Between our constant moves, changes in schools and hiding out in the house, I had no friends. I had my books which made things more bearable, but I was miserable most years and impossible my teenage years. We once had to move from a town and a school I really loved because I insisted on going to prom with guy whose father ran the local biker gang. Yeah. Idiot teenager, too much to drink and diarrhea of the mouth earned us our next visit from Witsec and us ghosting that town.

God. How I hated my life.

Mom died, I left the program and didn't know the continuing problems living as a Witsec kid generated.

They gave me a passport and a social security number but not a birth certificate. The passport was supposed to cover ID issues. It didn't. Not always, especially when someone wanted two forms of ID. A lack of continuous school records didn't impress college admission officers, and I was left to falling to my own devices to earn a living. Thank the Lord for my love of writing, the internet, and online freelance platforms. Now I had a thriving business, a robust client list and a job I could take on the road when I needed to.

But with the Clark cousins chasing me, I was not getting my work done. And if I didn't write, I didn't eat. I mean, I literally had about a week's worth of grocery money on my debit card, and that wouldn't get me far. I had to put down some serious words to get enough money to get out of here to my next shelter, wherever that would be.

Cole walked into the lodge with his face as grim as could be. With purpose, he walked to the front desk and punched in a number.

"Zain, I have to talk with you. Yeah, I think so...No, can't. Yeah, Ellie is still here. Okay, I'll do that."

The phone hit the cradle more solidly than I expected.

"Cole? Is everything okay?"

He poked his head around the corner to peer into the sunken great room of the lodge where I sat. "Yeah. Everything is fine. I'm going to keep the door locked though. Don't try to answer it yourself."

"What's going on, Cole? You're acting spooked."

"Nothing to worry about. Someone's been trespassing,

but it could just be neighborhood kids looking for a place with some privacy. Sometimes our hunting cabins are popular spots for teenage explorations. But sometimes, people come off the Appalachian Trail looking for food, so I'd keep the door locked."

I didn't like the sound of that at all.

"People?"

"Your basic mountain man, rage-against-civilization type. Homeless, mostly though, sometimes criminals on the run hide out in desolate places. There are shelters on the trail. Not homey but keeps the rain off you."

"Wow. I'd like to see it."

"You would? Are you into camping? Hiking?"

"I haven't done either, but anything new that helps to fill the reservoir of a writer's knowledge is helpful. You never know when a little detail will help flesh out a story."

"I like that you're willing to try new things," he said. Cole seemed to relax a bit more now, talking with me. But I'm still aware that he walked into the lodge highly spooked.

"You can say I was born trying new things," I replied.

The front door rattled.

"Damn it, Cole," rumbled Zain through the door.

"Zain? Didn't he just leave?"

"Yeah. He must have forgotten his lunch." Cole's eyes crinkled, and I knew he was lying. What was he hiding from me?

Cole stepped outside, further arousing my suspicions, and I decided to test out the crutches. I'd used them during my teen years after an unfortunate attempt at skiing, so I made my way to the door.

Cole hadn't shut the door, and he and Zain were in an animated discussion with Cole gesturing to one of the other cabins-the one I supposed the new guest was in. Zain nodded.

"I'll take care of it."

Cole started for the front door, so I moved in the direction of the bathroom.

"Hey!" said Cole as he entered. "What are you doing?"

"Need to use the bathroom."

"Oh."

"So, what's up with Zain?'

"Oh, he forgot a piece of equipment. I told him it was in the storage shed."

"Seems like a long way to go to get a piece of equipment."

"Do you need help getting to the bathroom?" Cole said. This abrupt change of subject confirmed Cole hid something from me. But it wasn't like I could make him tell me what.

"No. I'm fine."

"Hey, are you hungry? What about lunch?"

"I thought food wasn't part of the cabin rental."

He grinned at me. "That's true. But you're injured. We're civilly liable to make sure you don't injure yourself on our land again. And they do say the kitchen is the most dangerous room in the house."

"Well, as long as it's a legal thing," I said. He smiled at me with the broadest, heart-melting grin I'd ever seen.

"But 'they' are wrong," I said. "The bathroom is the most dangerous room in the house."

"Then I'll have to have a talk with my sources of information," he said. In a second, he was at my side and looking down at me. Damn, how can any one man be this gorgeous? He smelled of clean air, smoke and aftershave. The collision of these intoxicated me. "Maybe I should give you a hand in the bathroom. Just to make sure."

My knees weakened, and I clung desperately to my crutches to keep me upright.

"I really should take care of that myself."

"No," he said seductively, "I insist. I'll help you inside and then leave you to do your business."

"That's certainly above and beyond."

"Anything for my guests," he said in a voice so smooth it was like warm caramel sliding down a scoop of ice cream. All I wanted was for him to wrap his strong arms around me, so I could feel the strength of his body.

Cole put his arm around my waist to steady me as we made our way down the hall toward the bathroom. He opened the door, and I stepped forward but forgot and stepped on my twisted ankle. With horror, I fell forward and instinctively squeezed my eyes against the impending fall.

That never came.

Instead, Cole wrapped his arms around my waist and pulled me upright.

"Are you okay?" he said. His warm brown eyes were filled with concern as if my well-being was the most important thing.

"Yes, fine. Thanks," I said breathlessly. My heart flip-flopped as he held me against his taut body. I turned to face him. "Really, I've got this from here."

He smiled. "You sure? Because from where I stand, I've got you." Cole watched me with magnetic intensity as if he wanted to know every thought that crossed my mind.

Oh, I had thoughts. Wildly inappropriate ones where I stroked his cock to hardness, and put it in my mouth, and watched the expression on his face as I…

Stop. Just stop. I had to fight the strangled breath in my throat. Damn. This guy was so hot I was melting from the inside out, my brains along with my core, and I had to pull away before I did something incredibly stupid.

My heart did not get this memo as the delivery service from my brain to the rest of my body was short-circuited by Cole's sheer sexiness. He leaned his body achingly close to me, and his manly scent intoxicated me, and right at this moment, I wanted him to push me against the wall while I wrapped my legs around him. I didn't know what was happening to me, this lack of common sense, but I didn't care. He was just too damned delicious.

Electricity ran through me, driving a need to get closer to him as if our flesh was melting into each other now. My mouth may have parted inviting him to kiss me, which he did, slowly, purposefully, imparting a thousand promises that couldn't possibly happen. But I wanted to believe them, at least now, because I never wanted him to stop touching me.

The front door slammed open.

"Cole!"

Zain's voice projected through large space of the lodge, and Cole pulled away with regret in his eyes.

"Stay here," he whispered.

I did not want to let him go, but I did. Cole and Zain talked in hushed urgent tones, and then footsteps sounded on the floorboards coming towards me. Zain's hulking form filled the hallway.

"Come with me," Zain said as if his words brooked no argument.

"What's going on?"

Zain stepped forward and without preamble swept me into his arms.

"We have to get you out of here, now."

"**B**ackpack," I said gruffly to Cole who shook his head but went to the kitchen to get my pre-packed backpack. I opened the closet in the wall opposite the front door and pulled out an empty backpack.

"What is going on?" said Ellie. Her eyes narrowed, and it was obvious she wasn't happy, but I would to protect her.

Cole trotted to me.

"Arm," he rumbled unhappily and slung the backpack on my left shoulder.

"Where are you taking her," Cole demanded.

"You know where I'm going. Don't make me say it."

"Please do," said Ellie sarcastically. "I'd like to know where my kidnapper is taking me.

"Look," I said. "I just tossed off our property a man with a gun—a man whose ID did not check out. I don't know who he is, but he isn't here for the fishing."

Fear sparked in Ellie's eyes. "What does he look like?"

"Why, Ellie?" said Cole. "If someone is looking for you, we need to know."

"Yes," I rumbled in agreement. "We'll protect you. But you have to let us know what from."

Ellie looked away and bit her lip.

"Just get me on the bus, and I won't bother you anymore."

"Do you think it's that easy? Ellie, I'm not going to let you out on the road with someone after you."

"It's my business." Ellie's eyes glittered with determination, even though she lay in my arms. And curiously, I didn't want to let her go. She was a petite woman, almost nothing in my arms, yet her eyes burned with an intensity that cast a shiver down my spine and made me very aware of her presence.

Yes, it was her business. But curiously, it was my business too. Ellie showed up on my land on my watch, and there was no way I would let her come to harm.

"So, he's gone then." Cole said. His eyes glowered, and anger rolled off the normally jovial man.

I nodded. "Call Drew. Give him the information the man gave you when he registered and tell him to run it. Also let him know I'm taking 'personal time,' and to meet up at our spot tonight.

"All of us?"

"Yes. And put up the 'closed for the season' sign. We're shutting down until we get this cleared up."

"I'm glad you're taking this seriously."

I nodded. We are a territorial lot, and these unwelcome intrusions were wearing on my nerves. Sure, we got the odd teen pair of miscreants who trespassed for fun's sake. But this was different. First a known criminal and now an unknown with a firearm taking up residence until I kicked him out.

"Let's go," I said. I handed the empty backpack to Cole. "Bring up her clothes later."

"Now wait a minute," Ellie said struggling in my arms. "I

demand to know what you plan to do. Where are you taking me?"

"Full of questions," I rumbled. "I'll answer yours if you answer mine."

Ellie's lips drew a tight line. She wouldn't tell me anything.

No matter.

"I thought as much," I said and started for the door.

"Wait! My laptop."

"We will not have internet service where we are going," I said.

"I don't care about that. But I have work to do."

"Hmph. Cole, put her laptop in here."

"And my phone."

I scoffed, but Cole scrambled to where Ellie sat, and gathered her shoes and electronic equipment.

"Put the phone in the walk-in. Whoever is tracking her already knows she was here. The walls will block the phone's signal."

"Good idea."

"Yep. Open the door."

"Now wait a minute," protested Ellie.

"Is there something you want to tell me, Ellie? Anything to clear up why a gun-toting angler who didn't bring any fishing gear rented a cabin here?"

"You can't do this."

"I'm the sheriff in this neck of the woods. If I take protective custody of a material witness, no one will say anything. But if you can tell me a good reason why I shouldn't, tell me now."

Her eyes narrowed and her jaw set. I wasn't getting another useful word out of her until Ellie decided to speak. Stubborn woman.

I sprint out the door while Ellie spouted a string of invectives as we crossed the meadow that spread out to meet the lake and the woods that climbed the mountain. Ellie clung to my neck, bouncing in my arms, now curiously silent as I ran up the slope. I could make better time as a bear, but Ellie doesn't know that about us yet, and there was no way I reveal our true nature to her now. Not only was it universally disapproved, the timing couldn't have been worse.

We reached cabin number four, but this was not our destination. I had a more private, personal place in mind. Our family called it "the spot," and it was where a family member went if they wanted quiet time in a safe place. It's where we were that day our parents died, and we didn't know why our parents weren't making dinner for us when we returned.

I darted across the logging road and into the depths of the forest that we warn guests not to enter. Not that it was unsafe, but we didn't mark our territory here as thoroughly as on the Lodge lands proper, so some of the larger predators roamed undeterred by the territory scents of our shifter forms. This was our land but between our different jobs, none of us had the time to roam the entire area.

Ellie clung onto me tighter as the atmosphere grew darker with thickened, wild vegetation, and the ground grew more unsteady with layers of humus and wet leaves. I kicked up their earthy scent as I ran. Birds in the trees twittered their warning that there was a predator in their midst, and the crows chattered angrily that someone disturbed their quiet day.

The tinkling of falling water greeted my ears signaling we were close. I broke out of the forest to a clearing in the ring of green featuring a pool and waterfall. At one end of the pool, a beaver dam channeled the water creating the pool and allowed a small stream as egress for the water. Over the rock face, water tumbled in a sheet into the pool.

"Wow," said Ellie.

"Hang on. We're going to get wet for a second."

"Wha--"

There just wasn't any easy way to do this. I walked to the rock face and onto a ledge just under the waterfall. But the way isn't entirely clear, so I dashed forward through the edge of the falls and came out behind it into a wide cave. Over the years that Clarks had occupied this land, the family had built this cave into a cozy space.

We had a wood stove that vented through a pipe set in the rock and wicker furniture, padded with handmade cushions and pillows. In the further recesses of the cave was a memory foam mattress on the platform that had been constructed for sleeping bags. Cole brought it up a couple of seasons ago. It was a dry cave despite the water flowing above. Occasionally we'd find a critter taking up residence, but there isn't anything that wants to share with a bear, so they evacuate quickly when we show up. For teenagers, it was a wonderful place to hide out from the parents, and I believe Cole may have brought more than one woman here.

I whipped off the tarp over the sofa and set her down.

"How's that," I asked. Her scent filled my nose, and I closed my eyes as my cock twitched. I can't afford to be unprofessional now but all I wanted was to get inappropriate with her.

"This is something," she said looking around.

"Are you sure you're comfortable?"

"The sofa is a little, um, hard."

"Let's see what I can do." I went back to the bed and pulled out the pillows under the protective tarp and tucked them behind her back.

"How's that?"

She grimaced. "Still not comfortable."

"Here," I said. Sinking down next to her, I pull her to my chest. "How's that?"

"Zain," she breathed. "I—"

"Ellie, you don't have to say anything. Do you know how beautiful you are?"

She blushed. "I bet all the Clark men say that to all the girls."

"No, Ellie," I said softly in her ear. "To tell you the truth, we don't date all that much."

"But Cole--"

"Cole has his friends, but none of them are special. He could have had any number of women, but he didn't pick any of them."

"Oh."

"Are you comfortable?"

"You're comfortable. Almost like a teddy bear."

I chuckled. "No man wants to be compared to a child's toy."

"Then you don't understand the attention we lavish on our teddy bears."

"No?"

She shook her head. "We hold them close at night and kiss them."

"Little girls do that?"

"Big girls do that too," she said with a smile. With that she turned up her lips to me and stared into my eyes, and I saw something I never had before.

My mate.

I felt her heart beating and it moved in time with mine and holding her felt like the most perfect thing in the world. Her back pressed against my chest and my hand cupped her breast. Her nipple hardened, and I rubbed my thumb over it gently, earning soft moans.

"Ellie," I whisper. I can't help it. Her name is a song calling to my soul.

"Zain. Why do I want you so much?"

Her scent hung in the air, and I was peripherally aware that mine did too, perhaps stronger than usual. My shaft presses into the crease of her jeans, and inside my bear growled. There were too many clothes between us.

"Ellie, Ellie." It seemed to be all I could say. I kissed her neck, and nibbled her ear, and she made little sounds of pleasure that made me bolder. Gently, I push her aside.

"What are you doing?" she said.

"Ssh," I said. I slide to the floor on my knees and look up at her.

"You're so delicious, I need to taste you."

Her eyes widened as I unsnap her jeans and pull them off, revealing a white lace thong that barely covered her femininity. I kissed her mound gently and worked my tongue under the thin strip covering her pink flesh and lavish it with my tongue. She wriggled under me, and I slid my hands to place her legs on my shoulders and held her lips, lapping up her cream then seeking more of it.

Ellie groaned, and I pulled her to my mouth. She tastes so good I can't seem to get enough. My cock strained against my jeans, but I was so intent on her noises of pleasure, and how she jutted her hips against my face, I don't care. My tongue found her center and I slipped it in between her pink petals while my thumb massaged the nub hidden in the folds of flesh. Her back arched as her breathing sped up and she bucked on my tongue.

"Zain!" she called out.

Ellie sighed, and I lifted her legs, laid them on the couch then sat next to her and gathered her in my arms. She laid her head on my chest.

"Don't you want—?"

"Ssh," I said. "There's time for that. We'll be here for a while."

"You sure got this place all tricked out."

"It's the Clark family special spot. We come up here when we want alone time."

"So, is that what we're doing now? Getting alone time?"

"No. I'm keeping you in a safe place while we sort out the issues with trespassers."

She sucked in a breath.

"Issues? As in more than one?"

"I'm afraid so. There was the incident at the beach when you were with Cole, the guest at the cabin, and a trespasser I found at one of the hunting cabins."

"And this doesn't happen?"

"Not like this. Not this often and forgive me, but I do not believe in coincidences. It started when you arrived."

Ellie hung her head.

"I can't ever escape my past," she said sadly.

"What past?"

She took a deep breath. "The name I use now was given to me by Witsec.

"You're a protected witness?"

"No. Not anymore. I went in as a child. I left five days ago because they thought it would be okay. It wasn't. My father has been tracking me. It's why I came here. I thought his reach didn't come this far North."

"And your father is?"

But I knew the answer even before she spoke it. Now I understood why his face looked familiar when I saw his FBI photo. Sitting on my sofa is the daughter of Xavier Lane, president of the criminal motorcycle club, Satan's Sons.

"*5-10, 180 pounds, long gray hair which he pulls back in pony tail, wearing biker leathers, a jacket with a Satan's Son patch...*"

Zain's description of Xavier Lane rolled around in my head while I scanned the road for the criminal. Either he took off toward Canada, which was doubtful because of the heavy border security, headed south which seems counter-productive, or he was still hanging around here, which would be stupid. No one said criminals were smart; he's probably hanging around, maybe finding a shelter on the trail or in one of the parks to hole up in. He would need a warm place for the night, because May nights could get frosty until later in the month.

After filling my gas tank at the convenience mart across from the general store, I pulled up into a parking spot and took out my phone. I loaded up the local maps and mentally listed the places with shelters. I knew them all, and I would try to hit as many as I could. I sure wished I scented the bastard though. It would make it easier to find him.

Two hours of fruitless searching got me nowhere, and I

sat at the edge of a brook eating my sandwich wondering where to look next. My phone buzzed, and I found a message from Cole texting me from his emergency phone in his shifter's backpack.

Cole: Where have you been?

Me: Working.

Cole: Zain took Ellie to the spot.

Me: So?

Cole: He's *alone* with Ellie at the spot.

My mouth twisted. I did not like this, and my inner bear rumbled but what could I do? I had my shift to finish which wouldn't be for a while yet.

Me: I'm sure he's just trying to protect her.

Cole: DUDE! He's alone with Ellie at the spot!

Me: Chill.

Cole didn't answer while I chewed on my sandwich. No "bye." No "See you later." Why was he so upset about this?

The rumble of motorcycles greeted my ears. Any bright, sunny day will bring out the bikers. I finished up my sandwich in one bearish gulp and brush the crumbs off my fingers. I walked toward the parking lot and checked out the bikes—Harleys, of course, and catch a glimpse of their patches. No Satan Son's patch, just a single patch of a social club.

"Hey ya!" I said.

The bikers, six of them, looked at me and then at each other.

"Ya?" said the oldest one, a man with a beer gut, long gray hair and a beard.

"I'm Warden Clark. I wonder if you've seen any other bike clubs on the road."

"What clubs?" said the grizzled biker.

"Whoever you've seen."

"Nah. We haven't seen anyone."

"Okay. Thanks." I walked toward my truck, which was huge because of all the things I needed it for, and pulled open the driver's side door.

"Is there trouble?" called the biker.

"You told me there wasn't," I responded.

"What if we did see someone?"

"It's not a thing," I said. "I was just looking for someone, but I'll catch up with him."

The biker set his kickstand and walked toward me. His buddies followed, and I waited behind my door. I don't think they'll cause a problem, but I'll be ready to jump in if I need to.

"We don't want trouble," said the guy, whose front patch read "Digger," his club name, under the president's patch.

"I'm not looking for it, at least from you. You guys are a social club, right?"

"Yeah. We are. Weekend warriors most times, but this week we took a few days off to ride. It was a long winter."

"That it was," I agreed.

Digger looked over his shoulder to his fellows, a couple of whom shrugged.

"We," said Digger, "saw some assholes on the road. Normally we wouldn't say anything, and we don't want this to come back to us, but a group of Satan's Sons passed us on the way up. We haven't seen them since though."

"Assholes?"

"Yeah. Deliberately passed on the right spitting up sand for the shoulder. Jerks."

"On the road up here?"

"Yeah."

"How many?"

"Eight?" He glanced at his fellows who nodded.

I fished one of my cards out of my front shirt pocket. "You see anything else, I'd appreciate a call."

"Sure," grumbled Digger. He slipped the card inside his jacket and turned to his club mates. But I'm not worried about Digger; but Drew and Cole were a different story. Drew would be fine at the office, but Cole was alone at the lodge, and Xavier Lane already walked on our land once.

Not that my cousin couldn't take care of himself. He was a fierce bear when he shifted. But we didn't need crazy stories about humans that turned into bears.

I called my cousin, but damn it, the lodge answering machine picked-up instead of Cole.

The next call was to Drew.

"Hey," I said. "I just ran into a biker club that said they saw a group of Satan's Sons heading this way."

"Okay. I'll alert other law enforcement. Thanks for the tip."

"And Zain took Ellie to the spot."

"What!" I'm taken aback about the amount of alarm in his voice. "He can't do that."

"What's your dysfunction?"

"I don't want Zain hanging around my mate."

My blood literally runs cold through me.

His? His? The idea rattled in my brain, and my inner bear growled, ready to reach across the air waves to throttle my cousin. What the hell? The reaction was extreme, and my bear threatened to come to the surface because I haven't been listening to him.

With a shock, I realized what the bear has been trying to tell me.

"She can't be your mate."

"Why?"

"Because she's mine."

"Oh, hell, no. You are wrong there."

"No, bro. I am not. I felt the mate bond."

"This is bullshit," snapped Drew. "I've known she was mine since the first time I saw her."

It's a good thing I was sitting because the world tilts as I absorb this information. This was not right. Mates recognized each other, and the first of the bonds snap into place. But it doesn't happen where more than one bear shifter claims the same mate. Once the first mate bonds, the recognition forms, and no other bonds are possible.

Are they?

Then I thought bout Cole's overreaction to me telling him that Zain took Ellie to our secret spot to protect her.

Did he think Ellie was his mate too?

I felt sick. Suddenly my sandwich doesn't sit in my stomach. If this was true, there was only one thing I could do, and I don't know if I can.

I had to fight my cousins.

DREW

’m shaking when I hang up the phone after speaking to Marcus. My bear rumbled under my skin, ready to shift into my ursine form and rip the throat out of my cousin for daring to suggest Ellie is his mate.

That's not possible. She's mine. My bear was sure of it. I was too.

There was no way I could man that office. I shut down my computer because I'm going home—Zain be damned. I knew he was protecting her, but he didn't have to do it alone.

I pulled my keys out of my desk drawer as the door to office opened. The man who walked in was maybe 5' 9" and thin and lanky with dark hair and eyes. He bore a hard look on his face like he'd seen a lot of bad stuff in his life.

"Can I help you?"

"I'm looking for my sister."

I stepped to the counter and pulled out an intake form.

"And you are?"

"Simon Walters."

"I see. And your sister's name?"

"Ellie Walters."

I must act cool. This guy, whoever he was, was not Ellie's brother. Families share body chemistry and similar scents. This guy was nothing like Ellie. I kept writing.

"I see. And where does Ellie live? Not around here. I would recognize the name."

"Pennsylvania."

"There's quite a few miles between here and there. What makes you think she's here?"

"She's real pretty. People remember her. The guy at the bus station said she bought a ticket for here."

"When did she go missing?"

"Five days ago. Only I wouldn't call it missing. It's just she left without telling me."

"That's concerning, but not a matter for the Sheriff's office. She's an adult, right?"

"Yes."

"And there is no sign of foul play?"

He stood suddenly as he considered his answer.

"No.

"But I'm worried about her."

"I can see that. But unfortunately, there's nothing I can do. However, I'll take your contact information, and should we run across her we'll tell her you're looking for her."

The man grumbled, and I gave him the cop stare that said not to mess with me. He walked out the door and barely kept it from slamming. I growled. I don't know who he is but he's after Ellie, and he lied to me.

I dialed Zain's number but if he's in the cave, the cell isn't going to work. Cell service is spotty there. Growling with frustration, I hesitated until Mrs. Ahern pushed open the door.

"Hello, Drew."

"Hello, Mrs. Ahearn. I thought you were still sick."

"I'm better, and I should get after those tax bills that need to go out."

"Good. Because Zain is taking a personal day, and I need to go on the road."

"Go ahead. I'll take messages, or if anything important happens, I'll call you."

"Thanks! I'll have Cole make you a cobbler," I said. Mrs. Ahern arriving relieved me of the guilt of leaving the office. Zain still wouldn't be happy, but I'll deal with that. I grabbed my hat from the coat rack by the door.

"And look. There are some rough characters in town looking for a woman by the name of Ellie Walters. You haven't seen her or know anything about her?"

"Who, Drew?" she said with a smile.

"Bye."

I almost race to my truck and head back home. If I wasn't the Sheriff, I would have given me a ticket. Ten miles on country roads take a long time to travel, and my heart thundered in my chest. The sense of danger only increased for each mile I gained. My bear rebelled, wanting to run free toward the danger to save our mate, but I needed to rein him in.

Finally, I turned onto our private road leading to the lodge. I see dirt kicked up and the broad outline of Marcus' truck ahead of me. He was moving fast, as fast as me, and as soon as he pulled into his parking slot, I slid into mine.

He jumped over the rail fence that divided the parking lot from the broad lodge lawn. I followed.

"Wait up."

"Cole hasn't answered my call."

"Do you think there's trouble?"

He whirled, his face grim. "Of course, there is trouble, and it involves all of us and Ellie."

"The biker?"

"No," he snorted. "That's the least of our problems."

"Then what is it?"

"Ellie," he growled.

"What about, Ellie?"

"All of us think of her as our mate. All of us. Do you know what that means?"

I froze, and my bear fought once again to take over. My stomach turned as I held the beast in. I did know what it meant. Bears fought furiously for the right to mate. Our inner bears would want to do the same. But I couldn't imagine hurting a cousin as close as a brother.

"This is awful," I said.

"No more terrible than when we get to the spot, and we find Zain mated with Ellie."

"Let's find Cole," said Marcus. "We have to talk to him too."

I didn't have much hope that we could work this out amicably. Living on the land, stretches of letting our bears out to roam, relatively solitary lives, except for each other—all helped to keep our wild ursine natures under control. But this issue of who claimed Ellie as his mate could rip us apart. I had no idea how we were going to solve this problem without destroying our family.

I couldn't handle it. We lost our family, our clan, in a horrible accident, and all I had left were my cousins. Without them, I'd just shift and live as a bear for the rest of my life. I didn't want that, but my broken heart wouldn't let me live as human anymore.

And the worst part of this was that I would fight for Ellie, a woman I barely knew, because my bear recognizes her as the one true mate we'll ever have.

"This is wrong," I said to Marcus. "We are what's left of the Clark Clan. We have to find a way through this."

"How? Draw straws?"

"No. But there has to be a solution where we aren't tearing each other apart."

Marcus stood and rubbed his chin.

"We are looking at this the wrong way," he said. "We are acting like Ellie doesn't have a choice. But she does. We'll have to stand by her decision which one of us she wants."

"And if she doesn't want any of us."

"Then we'll have to live with that."

No, my bear grumbled. *Not allowed. She's ours.*

My hands tingled and my claws threatened to poke out of the ends of my fingers. I was losing control fast.

I can't let that happen. So that's why I run across the field, losing my clothes as I go, knowing I'm going to shift, heading away from a man as close as a brother, so I don't tear him apart.

C O L E

After talking with Marcus on the phone, I grabbed my emergency pack, set the security system and tore toward the wide meadow to the slope leading to the hunting cabins. I went over the logging road and dove into the woods, following the way to where Zain took Ellie.

Zain was our Alpha, but even an Alpha can't disturb a mating bond, and I wouldn't let him try. Ellie was mine, and even he had to recognize that.

I didn't believe I had to fight Zain, a man I considered my big brother, for my mate.

I might have overreacted, but I didn't think so. Marcus' response to when I claimed her told me that I was in danger of losing my mate to one of my cousins, and I couldn't allow that.

When I made the trees, I stripped and packed my clothes and my shoes in the backpack. Slinging it over my shoulder, I shifted and sprinted up the hill. My broad paws and long claws gripped the soft earth and tore at humus and leaves. I wasn't delicate because I was in a hurry, and I had a few

88

miles to go through rough territory before I reached Zain and Ellie.

I scented my alpha though Ellie's is nearly subsumed in Zain's. Growling, I quickened my pace and my backpack flopped on my shoulder. My breathing huffed with the pace in the rolling half-growl of bear on the hunt. Bears could be stealthy, but more often we don't care. Not much can escape us when we sight our prey. The power in our muscles trumps most any other animal's skill at flight.

At the top of the rise, I caught the sound of human voices, and I skid to a stop. Cabin Eight stood ahead and a number of men swarmed around it. I stood in a stand of underbrush, and my black fur hid me well. I studied them, six, swarming around the cabin, smoking pot and making crude remarks. They had kicked open the door and splintered the door jamb and that alone made me want to charge.

A couple had their backs to me. I saw the patch on the back of their jacket, and drew a deep breath. My bearish brain didn't want to read the letters, but just focused on the colors and smells rolling off these dangerous men, but I forced myself.

Satan's Sons.

Why does my brain tickle with this information? Zain, Marcus and Drew don't always share information about their law enforcement activities. Marcus was more likely to share stories about his job, seeing that mostly they involved some of the more ridiculous things that happened to him while he worked.

I'd heard of them somewhere, but I can't place where. But it's obvious they were criminals.

A few shouts came from the direction of the road, and four more men walked in from that direction. Or rather one grizzled old man walked in front of two other bikers who slung a man between them. With a sharp intake of breath, I discover it was our erstwhile renter, Orlando Cortez. The two men holding up his near unconscious and bloodied form frowned, and one swore.

"Where do you want him, boss?" said one.

"Put him in the cabin and tie him up. Rencher and Diamond, you guys take the shovels from the tool box and go dig a place we'll stick him."

Two beefy guys nodded, and one walked to the side where we kept a long box of tools. Each cabin had one, equipped with a rake and shovels for putting out small fires. I can only imagine what they did to it when they first came here, but their intent was clear. They would kill Cortez.

Zain had chased Cortez off, and we don't know his story. But he wasn't their friend, and these men were now my enemy. The enemy of my enemy is my friend.

There were eight of them, and one of me, and while I can do damage, I have no doubt these guys would hurt me as well. I'd need my clan mates to take on this threat.

I thought over my options, though I know I didn't have much time. Zain was another ten minutes away at a good clip. The lodge was five, but I don't know where Marcus and Drew were. And then, as if in answer to a prayer, I hear crashing in the underbrush and I whirl to meet them. Their familiar scents were welcome, but I had to get them to approach more quietly. I backed away, then turned and slid down the hill and nearly ran into Marcus and Drew.

I shifted and put my hand to my mouth to indicate they needed to be quiet.

"There's a biker gang, nine men, at Cabin Eight and they have our former renter, Orlando Cortez tied up. They're going to kill him."

Marcus huffed and nodded. He caught my eye and jerked his head to the right and looked to Drew and jerked his head to the left. I knew what he wanted so I shifted once again.

We took our positions stealthily. Our ursine forms stole the dusky dark of the forest for our camouflage. Drew circled to the left flank, me to the right, and Marcus would charge from the center. And we had to do it quickly before any of these criminals thought to pull a gun to shoot at us.

Marcus let out a roar, and we rushed forward. One guy in my direct path looked up at me in surprise, dropped the joint from his mouth and screamed. One swipe of my paw sent him into the cabin. Screams, shouts, curses and groans of pain filled the air as my cousins and I fought this blight on our land.

There may have been nine of them, but they were no match for the three full grown bears with teeth and claws as sharp as daggers.

"Let's get out of here," screamed the grizzled man, and he ran toward the road. His gang followed, with some grabbing and hauling their two most injured members.

In all of this I managed to hang onto my backpack, so I shifted and dressed.

"Go," I said to Marcus and Drew who stared at me with bearish eyes. "Get that filth off our land. I'll take care of Cortez."

Marcus and Drew flew after the trespassers and I opened the door half-dreading what I would find. Cortez sat in the middle, bound and tied, looking as mad as a hornet.

"Hey," I said, as I pulled out his gag. "Are you okay?"

"What happened?" he sputtered.

"We ran them off," I said.

"I thought I heard roaring, like bears."

"Yeah," I said, lying through my teeth. "Marcus has this bear call. It comes in handy sometimes. So, you gonna tell me why those men had you prisoner."

He sighed, pissed and unhappy. "I've been following them. I'm FBI. My badge is in my wallet."

I pulled it out of his back jeans pocket and found the ID.

"So, you are. You know you would have spared us some trouble if you told us what you were."

"I didn't know who I could trust. After all, you had his daughter staying at your hotel."

"It's a lodge, not a hotel. And I'm not sure I know what you mean." I pulled out my cellphone and gratefully found I got cell service here. I dial 911 to pick up Cortez and get him to a hospital.

"Ellie Harper is the daughter of the president of Satan's Sons MC club, Xavier Lane."

I just stared at him until the dispatcher came on the line, and I arranged the transport for Special Agent Orlando Cortez.

Zain brought me outside, so I could dangle my feet in the pond. The chilly water soothed the residual pain in my ankle, though to tell you the truth, the ankle was feeling much better. It was a lovely warm day and sitting outside in the sun relaxed me. That and Zain's tender ministrations which put a smile on my face.

Thrashing and flailing branches in the undergrowth picked up my attention.

"Zain?" I called. Pulling my feet out of the water I scooted back.

"What?" said Zain.

"Something is over there. An animal I think."

Zain's face crinkled in concern, and he drew in a breath.

"It's not an animal. Cole! What are you doing here?"

Cole's blond hair shone in the sunlight as he stepped out of the brush. "Hey, Ellie," he said with a bright smile.

"Cole?" said Zain in a warning voice.

"I have to talk to you."

"So do we," said Marcus and Drew, walking from the

brush. They didn't smile as broadly as Cole did, and all three stood in a line as if challenging Zain.

"What's going on?"

"We chased off a bunch of trespassers from the land," said Marcus. "They took off on the bikes before we could catch them."

"But we roughed them up good before they got away," said Drew.

"Don't tell me, Satan's Sons."

I groaned.

"I'm so sorry," I said mortified. I suspected my father was tracking me, but I honestly thought that I had outrun him. "Did any of you get hurt?"

"You have nothing to be sorry for," said Marcus. "And no, we didn't get hurt. But a certain FBI special agent whose been on your trail is in a hospital now getting a good work-up."

"FBI?"

"Yeah," growled Drew. "He thought by following you it would lead him to your father. Instead the agent led your father to you. And what kind of bonehead move is that, leaving WITSEC?"

"You don't know what it's like," I said. "I had no life. After my mom died, I decided I deserved one."

"You might have told us a little more, so we could protect you better," said Cole.

"I don't expect you to protect me."

"Zain, have you explained nothing to her?"

"And what am I supposed to tell her that doesn't sound bat-shit crazy?"

"Well," said Cole, "it's going to get crazier."

"What do you mean?"

"She's going to have to decide," said Marcus.

Zain's mouth opened, then closed, apparently befuddled by the logic of a conversation I do not understand.

"We all think of her as ours," said Cole.

"Now wait a minute!" I said. "I don't belong to anyone."

"That," said Drew, "is where you are wrong."

"Drew," said Cole in a low voice, "be careful."

"No, I don't think so," he said as he started to strip. "She doesn't understand, and she's not going to until she knows everything."

I watched wide-eyed as Drew took off his clothes and stood before me naked. Zain stood between me and him, so I didn't think I'd come to harm. But then his body changed, and I watched opened-mouth as the gorgeous man I knew as Drew sprouted a thick growth of hair and then claws. I'm transfixed, unable to move in my shock.

"What are you? A werewolf?"

Despite the incredulous scene, Zain, then Cole and Marcus laughed.

"No hardly, sweetheart," said Cole. "Though some might call us werebears."

"Us?"

"All of us," affirmed Marcus.

My head swam especially as Drew ambled to me and pushed his snout into my shoulder. I blinked, and the world swirled around me.

The next thing I knew, I was laying in a bed, and I recognized the cave walls and four very concerned men stood around me.

"I'm sorry," said Drew.

"I warned you to be careful," said Cole.

"Recriminations do no good," said Zain.

"Maybe I should get on my way," I said.

Marcus sat at the edge of the bed. "Are you sure you want to leave?"

My heart shredded then, because, no, damn it, I don't want to leave. But this is all too crazy—men turning into bears.

"Ellie," said Zain. "I have to tell you, your father is still out there, but we can keep you safe."

"Against a criminal motorcycle gang?"

"We did today," said Marcus. "We ran them off."

"This is too much." I covered my face with my hands. "I'm not a crying type of gal, but I'm almost there now."

"Ssh," said Cole, sinking on the bed next to me on my left and laying a gentle kiss on my cheek.

I don't know what to do. I'm just so tired of running from place to place, of not having a safe place to be.

Marcus sat behind me. "You don't need to make any decisions now. We want you to stay, Ellie."

Cole sat at the leading edge and stroked my feet, sending wonderful tingles up my legs.

"The problem, Ellie, is that we all want you. Us bear shifters do things a little differently. When we find our mate, the other half of our souls, we know it. But we all feel the same way. We decided that you can pick one of us or none of us."

"We did?" said Zain.

"Hey, don't blame us if you didn't read your memos," said Cole.

Zain gave a low snarl, though I found it kinda cute the way he did it. I glanced at each of the men, and my heart sank. How can I choose between any of them? I like them all. Maybe a little more than that.

I shook my head. "I can't choose between you."

"Crazy thought," said Cole. "Take all of us."

"That is crazy? Four guys."

"You know," said Drew. "That might work. I mean, we literally share everything else."

"I'd rather," said Marcus stroking my hair, "have my mate around, than taking off because we've given her an impossible choice."

"What?" I scoffed in a squeak. I turned and gave a hard stare to his bemused eyes. "You don't think much of yourself, do you?"

"Ellie," said Zain. He took my hand and kissed it. "Before you showed up, we were four lonely bears with each other for company. And we didn't realize how lonely we were. But you're here now, and you're so precious. You just don't know how much. And I promise - each of us promises, to make your days as happy as possible. You deserve it for the happiness you bring us."

I think I'm going to melt. No one has ever said such sweet things to me. As I looked at each man, Cole, Drew and Marcus, each gazed at me so lovingly that I thought my heart might explode.

"What's going to happen now?"

"I think," said Cole, "that we should explore this new relationship in all its permutations."

"Cole," said Drew, "you are devious man."

"I prefer adventuresome and believe me, this will be an adventure - if you want to, Ellie."

"What do you have in mind?"

"Umm," said Marcus with long lick up my spine that made me shiver. "This."

Drew cupped his hand on my breast. "And this."

Cole leaned forward and kissed my mound. "This, mmm."

"And," said Zain. He leaned over me and took a nipple in his mouth and sucked on it hard.

And I would be lying if I said that having four hot men in bed with me didn't turn me on. Because I was lit like a Christmas tree and every part of my body tingled and sparked as they licked me in every way possible. I floated into a world of sensation somewhere between Drew nibbling the inside of my elbow and Marcus licking behind my ear. Zain claimed my mouth with a hot kiss that stole the breath out of me.

Marcus rose for a minute, and I whimpered from the loss of him. But he returned quickly, sat against the headboard, and hitched me on his lap. His thick, hard cock pressed into the crease of my butt. Marcus pulled me up and pressed the head of his cock to my slit, splitting me in half.

"You're so tight," he gasped. He held my hips as I rode him, pulling me down hard, filling me, and each plunge lifted me higher. I opened my eyes to see Zain, Cole and Drew staring at me and Marcus, pulling on their shafts, eyes blown with lust. It was the hottest thing I'd ever seen, and I fell over the edge, white stars flying through my body and before my eyes.

Our mate was beautiful and seeing how we all brought her pleasure made everything right. Cole, Drew, and Marcus, cousins by blood, were my brothers in my heart. How could I not love all of them and her together?

I didn't know what the future would bring, but we had to get these bikers off the road, and Xavier Lane in jail. I wasn't sure how Ellie would feel about that, but there didn't seem to be love lost between them.

As we all cleaned quickly with water from the cold pond, I spoke up.

"They'll be back," I said. "Lane was here twice, this second time with friends. We have to go after them."

"No," said Marcus. "He'll be back for her".

I shook my head because what Marcus was thinking was not how we were going about it. "No way are we setting her up as bait."

"I don't think you can avoid it," Ellie said. "If you expect me to stay here, then we're going to have to let him come to me and deal with him then."

My cousins grumbled, and I agreed with the sentiment. But she also made sense, damn it. Putting her in danger, though, went against the grain.

"Then let's go to the lodge and wait it out."

"He'll know we're there?"

"We'll turn on all the lights," said Cole, "and fire up the main fireplace to send up a smoke signal from the chimney. The whole valley will know the Clarks are home."

The late afternoon sun slanted through the darkening treetops as we walked into the lodge. Drew, Marcus and I spread out and checked the property around the house to make sure no one broke in while Ellie stood on the porch biting her nails. I wanted to reassure her that everything would be fine. But she probably knew better than we did the type of criminal we were dealing with. From what Marcus said, they were going to kill that FBI agent Cortez.

Once we got inside, Drew set the fire, Cole and Marcus busied themselves with pulling dinner together, and I motioned for Ellie to join me on the couch.

"Come sit with me," I said, and she sighed and snuggled next to me."

"Don't get too comfortable there," said Drew. "I'll be there in a minute."

"You can try," I said with a smirk.

Ellie slapped my arm. "Stop."

"Sassy? Are you being sassy?" I rumbled in her ear.

"Yes."

"Good. I like it. Drew, go check the perimeter."

"Let a guy get a couple sandwiches first. We'll hear their bikes if they arrive."

Her face saddened. "How is this all supposed to work out?"

"We'll take it one day at a time."

"Don't let him put you off," said Drew. "He can take a while making a decision."

"Drew," I growled.

"Yeah," said Cole, coming from the kitchen carrying a plate of sandwiches. "Zain's decision tree is tall."

"Don't 'dis your Alpha," I said.

"I like your tall tree," Ellie murmured in my ear. She smiled, and sunshine filled my chest despite the situation we were in.

An inappropriate comment about her tasty bush stuck in my throat. I'm sure it wouldn't be appreciated now. I kissed the top of her head.

"So, tell us about your father."

Marcus walked into the room holding beers and handed them out to us.

"I was little, no more than seven, when the Witsec agents showed up and took us away. I didn't understand why, but my mom was afraid, and I didn't have much choice. I learned years later that Mom went to them and said she had information if they would protect us. Turns out the government couldn't make their case against him, though they got a few of his lesser soldiers. When my mom was in court, he threatened her life. After that we moved so often I don't remember all the towns we lived in, though during my teenage years, it wasn't as often. When my mom died a couple months ago, I decided to get out. He wanted her, not me. At least that is what I thought."

"With what Marcus witnessed," I said. "We have him cold on conspiracy to commit murder. If he shows up, we'll arrest him."

"And then what? He has a nationwide network of bikers who will do anything he says. You four will always be in danger."

"Hey," said Marcus with a wide grin, "If I can survive a trapped deer, I can handle anything."

"It was a fawn," said Cole.

"Deer. Fawn. Both have sharp hooves."

Ellie bit her lip, and consternation filled her face.

"There are hundreds of them, and four of you."

"The odds sound about right," said Drew.

"You let us worry about Xavier Lane and Satan's Sons," I said. "Here, have a sandwich." Ellie shook her head, and my bear rumbled his disapproval. I hold up the sandwich again.

"Let her be, Zain," said Cole.

"Fine," I said, tearing into it.

"What was that?" said Drew. "I thought I saw lights outside.

All four of us stood.

"Take her to the bathroom, Cole."

"What?" Why?" said Ellie.

"It has no windows," I said. "It's the safest room on this floor."

"Come," said Cole. "With you safe, these guys can do what they do best."

A loud bang shot through the room, and the glass from the window next to the door shattered, spraying shards through the room. I pushed Ellie's head down, as the door flew open.

"Back to the hall," I shouted. We needed a defensible choke point, and the hall was the best place.

Cole pulled Ellie back toward the hall as men poured in the front door. Marcus, Drew and I looked at each other. We couldn't shift or these men would witness our secret. We all dove behind the long couch that sat in front of the fireplace, though it wasn't a great defensible location, since it was a sunken living room. I pulled on the top of the couch and getting the idea, Drew and Marcus followed. We flipped the great piece of furniture on us. I had the idea that if we had cover we could shift, and it would have worked but for the bullet that winged my shoulder causing me to fall and hit my head.

MARCUS

Fuck. Watching Zain fall was a shock. He was breathing, and while he was bleeding that wouldn't last long. Our shifting abilities by virtue of rearranging muscle, bone and sinew gave us extra-fast healing abilities. I was more concerned that he was knocked cold, but I can't think about that. About six of Satan's Sons stood inside our lodge now with their guns trained on us.

Drew sucked in a breath when a man that fit Xavier Lane's description strolled in. He sneered at us and we let go of the couch to thud it back into position.

"Where's Ainsley?"

"I don't know an Ainsley," I said.

He snorted. "Ainsley!" he called. "Come see your daddy."

"I told you. There is no Ainsley here."

Lane nodded his head to one of his men who pulled the trigger to send a shot whizzing by my head.

"No!" cried Ellie, and I closed my eyes for a second. "Leave them alone!" She ran out of the hall shaking off Cole and skidded to a stop to face Lane.

"What do you want?" she snapped. "Why are you bothering me? Why are you following me?"

Lane's face hardened, and I could see that this is not the right tack to take with him.

"They took you from me, Ainsley."

"You're a criminal."

"Who told you that? Your mother? Faithless whore."

"Don't talk about my mother. She didn't run drugs and guns and whatever else you got your hands on."

"She poisoned you to me. The things she said I did, I didn't."

"Liar!"

"They couldn't make their case against me."

"No. Other people went to jail for you. In any case, I want nothing to do with you."

"Too bad. Where's your mother?"

"She's dead, asshole," Ellie said with vehemence. "You worried her to death."

He chuckled, and Ellie's expression betrayed the depths of her anger toward Lane.

"Spitfire. Like your mother. So, the witch is dead."

"I said shut up about my mother."

"Where's her locket?"

I hadn't thought about it, but Ellie did wear a locket. Her tee shirt covered it now.

Lane stepped forward, closer to Ellie, and she backed away.

"I don't know," said Ellie defiantly. "I don't remember a locket."

"No. She had it. I saw it that day in court. Other times too, when I got close. Of course, she'd find out somehow, and you'd be gone in a couple hours. Clever of her to keep Witsec moving her around. Now, Ainsley, the locket. Or your friends will suffer for it."

Ellie glanced at us and sucked in a breath when she saw

Zain unconscious and bleeding on the floor.

"Then you'll leave and not bother us again."

"Oh, we'll leave. Give me the locket, Ainsley."

With inching slowness, Ellie unclasped her necklace then handed it to Lane. With a grin, he pried open the back, and a key fell into his hand.

"Very good. Okay, come along, Ainsley." He turned to walk out the door.

"I'm not going anywhere with you."

"Which one of your friends do you want to die first?" he said. "Come, we have a long journey before we get to the bank that has the safety deposit box holding the money she stole from me. And since she isn't here to claim it, it's going to have to be you."

"Don't do it," called Cole.

Lane glanced at him as if Cole was a bug not worth the biker's time. "Do you want him to die first, Ainsley?" he said with a sneer.

"Don't hurt him. Don't hurt any of them."

"I don't see where I have a choice."

"Then kill me too, because if you do a single thing to harm them I will not go with you."

"Ellie," said Drew. "You don't have to do this."

Her face was heartbreakingly sad.

"I told you he wasn't going to leave us alone. I have too. Goodbye. Tell Zain, it was all wonderful."

"No, Ellie!" cried Cole.

I stood and watched all that was our life crumble away as Ellie walked out the door escorted by two of Lane's goons. How could she do this? How could we let her?

"Now," said Lane. And the four men standing next to him opened fire, hitting me, Drew and Cole as we ducked and turned, looking for a way to avoid the bullets. The last thing I remember hearing is Ellie's screams.

DREW

Pain shot through my body as I woke. A chilly wind streamed through the smashed-out window that displayed the night sky. Then a shadow stood over me.

"How are you?" rumbled a thoroughly-displeased Zain.

I forced my eyes open and groaned as I remembered Ellie getting dragged away by Lane's bikers.

"Ellie," I said miserably. "They have Ellie."

"Marcus and Cole told me."

I held my pounding head in my hand and scanned the room. Marcus and Cole weren't here.

"Where are they?"

"Scouting the property and looking for Ellie."

I sat up with a groan.

"Man, what did they do to me?"

"Gunshot. Grazed the head, nicked your ear. It's healed there, mostly. There's a notch in your earlobe."

"Fabulous," I said rubbing my ear. "What's the plan?"

"We're going to get her. And then we'll call the FBI and

clean this scum out. I've called Cortez and let him know what happened. He'll call people he knows in Witsec to see if they know anything about Lane's alleged missing money and where it might be. FBI's on the case, but I figure that it's safer for Ellie if we get her out before the FBI catches up with them."

"I'm with you." Zain held out a hand and helped me up. He looked fine, and probably on his next shift the bullet in his shoulder will pop out.

"How's your head?" I asked. "You were knocked out cold."

Before he could answer, Marcus and Drew burst in the shattered doorway.

"I got a call," said Marcus, "from another group of bikers I caught up with yesterday. They saw Satan's Sons about thirty miles south. They didn't get far in the dark last night."

"Let's go," said Zain strapping on his gun.

The drive south was grim, and we barely spoke. The events of last night played out in my head. I should have gone out on patrol when Zain told me, but I thought he was just trying to steal some extra time with Ellie. Looking back, I just didn't want to leave Ellie's side, which was common with a mate bond. My parents were like that, following each other around the house, and since I was a kid, I didn't think anything about it. Now, I understood exactly how they felt.

But that doesn't absolve me of the guilt that gnaws at my gut. I let myself get distracted, and we all suffered. But what's worse was that Ellie was in the hands of a maniac.

How stupid could we be?

The miles rolled under us, and the moon rose. I looked out over my shoulder to stare at the pale orb with its smiling ghostly face, neither male nor female, staring down on the earth. On a night like this, being derived from nocturnal black bears, we'd shift and prowl the woods to hunt or fish.

Walking under the moon, with only our thoughts and our paws padding the earth centered us.

Marcus scowled at his phone as we traveled, trying to figure the most likely place they would be. He called the numbers of the few campgrounds in the area, waking up sleepy campground owners.

"Got it!" he said. "A group of ten registered at the Happy Trails campground."

Zain's face grew grimmer as we sped down the highway.

"We're going in, getting her, and leaving them to the authorities."

Nervous anticipation knotted my stomach, and anger fired through my veins. How dare these men walk on our property and take our mate? I growled.

"Easy," said Zain. "Save it for the bikers."

We slid in slowly with the lights off into the entrance of the camp. Technically still the off-season, it was nearly empty, and in the distance through the scattered tree trunks do we see a flickering fire.

Zain stopped in front of the main building, a log cabin with a broad porch that sat at the fork of two dirt roads that ran around either side of it. He turned the truck to face the driveway.

"I'll be right back. I'm going to inform the owners what's going on. Get ready."

I couldn't be more ready. From the expressions on their faces, Marcus and Cole were too.

The minutes ticked by, and Cole shifted in his seat. Marcus drummed his fingers on his thigh.

"This is taking too long."

"We can't take the chance of exposing the owners to danger," I said.

"I know, but what if there is a problem?"

"Give him a few minutes. If Zain was in trouble, we'd hear about it."

Cole grumbled and opened his window. The whine of it resounded in the air around us.

"Quiet," I said.

Cole grumbled and stuck his head out of the window, then pulled his head back in. "Nothing. I scent nothing."

"You mean Ellie," asked Marcus.

Cole nodded.

Suddenly the truck door opened, and Zain climbed in.

"Okay, I told the owners what we want to do, and we have their permission to search the premises. They didn't like them when they showed up, but now that they know who they are, they want them gone. I told them to lock and bar their doors and windows and to get into the basement. I'll call them when things are clear."

We nodded and waited for Zain to give us the signal to start.

"The bikers are the only occupants of the campground, so that fire to our right is them. Marcus and Drew, you'll shift and flank their sides. Cole, circle around the back in human form to find Ellie and get her away. If you can head to the truck, fine. If not, hold out in a safe corner.

"Right," he said.

"I charge the front. Hopefully they are asleep, and we'll surprise them."

"Damn straight," said Marcus. "Trying to kill an FBI agent, shooting up the area law enforcement, kidnapping, and fleeing the scene of crimes is a tiring day's work. They should be out cold."

"Let's hope," said Drew as he stripped.

Cole slid out of the truck and made his way toward the campfire giving the area a wide berth. He's an awesome woodsman, and stealthy as a man or bear. Zain counted on his abilities here to get to Ellie quietly and safely. We gave him time to get there as we took off our clothes, and in the moonlit dark, slid into the shadows to make our way toward the biker's camp.

COLE

I knew why Zain sent me to get Ellie. He, Drew and Marcus thought I couldn't fight, at least not as well as them. But I wouldn't argue with my Alpha because I wanted Ellie back at home and safe.

The backpack with my cousin's clothes and the zip ties Zain had put in it clashed against the bushes, and I pulled it tighter to me to keep as quiet as I could. I'll drop it at the back of the tent, so they can grab their clothes after they take care of business.

Laurel bushes rose in clumps between the camping spaces acting as defacto fencing. The base and limbs of these bushes were strong and I had to work around them to get to the campsite. When I arrived, I positioned myself at the back of the campground's tent. I dropped the backpack as arranged myself and scented for Ellie. My nose lead me forward, and I spotted her, sitting with her head bent on her knees on a log next to the fire. The gang was there too, drinking beer, apparently well-conditioned to a life of crime. But they weren't my concern. I smelled my cousins nearby, and I heard the tell-tale rustling of their bear bodies brushing against the laurels and other bushes.

They were waiting for me to get Ellie out of danger. I picked up a pebble and sling it at Ellie's back. Instantly she snapped her head up, and looked in the darkness, but her human eyes couldn't see me, and her human nose couldn't smell me. She turned back, and I hit her with a pebble again. This time, she stood.

"Where do you think you're going?" said Lane.

"I need to use the bathroom."

"Go in the bushes. We aren't hiking to the latrines."

"Pig," she snorted.

He laughed. "Your mother liked that about me."

Ellie scoffed. "Yah, you being so charming and all." Indignantly she stomped into the darkness.

"Don't go so far away," growled Lane. "Rencher, go with her."

I growled in my throat because I remembered Rencher from earlier today. If he'd laid his hands on my Ellie, I would have gutted him.

I followed around behind the tent and make a wide arc swinging south to intercept them.

"Wait up, bitch," said Rencher.

My gut clenched because I'd lost sight of her, and I don't know what Rencher would do to her. But when I finally saw her again, she's standing with a thick branch in her hand while Rencher crashes through a laurel bush, ready to do him damage.

"What the—" starts Rencher before Ellie swings at his head with all her might.

Rencher is strong though and catches the branch and pushes back hard, throwing Ellie to the ground. I growled deep within my chest which brought Rencher's gaze to me and I leapt.

"Cole!" screamed Ellie.

We may look like normal humans, but our bear strength enlivens our muscles. I crashed on the biker dragging him to the ground. He thrashed under me and got off a few good shots to my jaw. His face turned to pure terror as I just grinned at him when his punches found his target and I didn't react.

"What the hell are you?" Fear dripped from his voice as I sat on his chest and held down his shoulders.

"Your worst nightmare."

"I've seen worse than you."

Ahead of me, I hear the growls of my cousins and the bikers' curses and screams.

"What?" said Rencher as he twisted his head to the screams.

"Nothing you need to worry about now. You'll soon be seeing the inside of a jail cell."

Rencher, having fewer brain cells than sense, scoffed at me.

"Night, night, Rencher," I said. With a hard-right cross, I knocked him unconscious and stood.

Ellie flew into my arms. "Cole!" She crushed her lips to mine, kissing me passionately. Okay. I don't envy my cousins now, because I'm holding Ellie and it was like I came home.

She pulled away. "But, oh my god, how is this possible. I saw—I heard—"

"You saw and heard four shifters getting shot. But little things like bullets may stop us temporarily but we're hard to kill."

She stared at me in amazement. "You're okay," Ellie said dumbfound. "And Zain, I saw Zain—"

"Alive, well and as bossy as ever."

"And Drew and Marcus?"

"Drew has a little nick on his ear that may repair itself after a shift or two. Darling, we're just *very* hard to kill."

"So, what are we going to do?"

"Zain wants me to get you back to the truck."

She shook her head.

"I want to see my father."

"It's not likely to be pretty up there. Zain, Marcus, and Drew attacked in bear form."

"Hah!" she said. "Still. I have some things I want to say to him."

I shrugged. "Okay." After slinging the unfortunate Rencher on to my shoulder, we walked back to the campsite where we found the bikers sitting with their hands zip-tied behind them, looking bruised and angry.

Marcus and Drew, dressed, stood over the men, all but Xavier Lane.

"Where's my father?" said Ellie.

"He ran away."

"Figured."

"Zain went to get him. He'll bring him back in a minute."

Crashes through the brush announced the arrival of Zain, hauling Lane roughly through the underbrush. Lane cursed and twisted like a snake in Zain's grip, but Zain kept pulling despite the branches whipping in Lane's face.

"I'll sue you," screamed Lane, "for excessive force."

"What excessive force?" said Zain. "From what I can see we saved you from a bear attack. You really need to be careful in the woods. Bears will come after any food you have. I can't help it if you ran through the brush to try to escape them. But now that I have you, I recognize you and your crew as the criminals who invaded my home and kidnapped my girlfriend."

"Your girlfriend?" shrieked Lane. "She's my daughter."

"You haven't been my father," said Ellie coldly, "for fifteen years, not when Mom had to run because you're a vicious and violent criminal. And if you come near me again, Zain, Marcus, Drew and Cole won't put up with it. So, do yourself a favor. Don't. Zain, the key is in his pocket."

Zain patted down Lane who scowled and retrieved the key but also took his personal possessions and put them in an evidence bag from his uniform pocket.

"Don't think this is the end of this," snapped Lane.

"Did I not tell you," said Drew, "that you have the right to remain silent? I suggest you exercise that right because what you say can and will be used against you. Do you want to add threatening on top of conspiracy to commit murder, kidnapping, and resisting arrest?"

Lane scowled. "Ainsley, it's not like what you said. Your mom turned you against me."

"My name isn't Ainsley, not anymore. And that's your fault. For all the years I had to run, to hide from you, that's what turned me against you. You should have just let it go. Instead, whatever safe deposit box that key opens was more important than your daughter's piece of mind. You should have let me have a decent life, then I would have known you cared."

She slipped her arm around my waist.

"Someone coming to pick these guys up?"

Zain nodded. "And to take our statements. I'm afraid it's going to be a long night."

"That's okay," she said glancing at each of us. "When this night is over, we'll start a new life."

"Go ahead, Ms. Walters," said Agent Cortez. "You can open it."

We stood at the bank that held the Massachusetts Bank's safe-deposit box that my father was after. Depending on what was in it, the contents may or may not be confiscated. My lips made a tight line as I fingered the edges of the lid. A part of my past was in that box, but what part, I didn't know. My father seemed to think it carried a ton of money, but the gray box on the table was too small to hold that kind of cash.

Zain, Marcus, Drew, and Cole stood behind me.

"Go ahead, sweetheart," said Zain gently.

I swallowed hard and lifted the lid to find two yellowed-with-age letter-size envelopes. One was addressed to me. And the other to my father.

Cortez snapped pictures with his camera.

"Open the envelopes," he instructed.

I pried apart the one addressed to my father. The glue was so old it came apart easily. I opened the letter:

. . .

Xavier,

If you got here and picked this up, that means I'm dead, and you got the key. But you won't find what you're looking for. Your ill-gotten money I gave to the FBI a long time ago. I know you wouldn't kill our daughter as you promised to do to me, but so help me, if you've harmed one hair on her head, I'll haunt you forever.

Leave her alone. You forfeited being a father a long time ago.

Marian

"Is that true? Did my mother give the money to the FBI?"

"Yes, she gave it over as evidence. But we thought there might have been more."

My throat thickened, and tears edged my eyes. What my mom went through. Apparently, she suffered eternal suspicion that she withheld evidence. I got a little angry now, because it seemed like she tried to do the right thing and did nothing but suffer for it.

I opened the second. This one was a little thicker and carried a handwritten note and my birth certificate.

Darling daughter,

If you are here, then I'm gone, and your father has finally been put away for his crimes. I am so, so sorry for how difficult things were for you. I wish I could tell you how many times I cried for you because of the bad choices I made. My sins were visited on you, and it wasn't fair. Please forgive me.

Here is your birth certificate. With it, you can change your name to anything you want and not what some government bureau cooks up for you. I hope the rest of your life is happy and that you find a good man.

Love always,

Mom

I held it and my hands shook.

"I did, Mom," I whispered. "Four of them."

Zain took the letters and laid them out on the table for Cortez to photograph. The flash on his iPhone was brief.

"Are you satisfied, Agent?" said Zain. "There's nothing here for you."

"You're right, Sheriff Clark. Thank you, Ms. Walters, for your cooperation. The prosecutor will be in touch with you to discuss court dates."

"Thanks," I said as Zain held me tight to his chest. This event had drained me emotionally, and all I wanted to do was to go home with my men.

Cole went to close the lid when he stopped and fingered something in the corner.

"What's this?"

"Hmm," said Marcus. He pulled out a nail file from his wallet and pried at something there. With a pop, metal struck the bottom of the safe-deposit box.

"I'll get the bank clerk," said Drew.

In a few minutes, a second box was opened, and I found a brief note:

Daughter,

This is from your grandma. She had some money and wanted you to have it.

All my love,

Mom

It was a bank statement in my original name with $500,000 in it, dated over 15 years ago.

"Oh geez, do you think the account is still good?" I said.

"We'll find out," said Marcus. "Even if it went to the state though, it's always there for you to claim."

Cole lost his sunshiny smile.

"I guess that means you have enough money to go anywhere you want."

"Sure," I said. "I guess I'll just think about it. I have to wait until after the trial anyway, don't I? That is if you guys don't mind me hanging around for a while?"

I guess I shouldn't have said that, because if there is anything worse than one grumpy bear, it's four. But as much as I loved all of them, a part of me, the little-girl-on-the run part said not to trust any of this. My world had been unstable for too long for me to promise forever even if they were the greatest guys in the world.

The other sheriffs and conservation officers were great filling in when necessary, so we could attend our various court dates while my father's trial went on. A year had passed since he was arrested, and it took time to get him to trial.

Zain, Marcus, Drew, and Cole improved the security system on the land around the lodge, so we had a better heads-up on who wandered onto the property. We all felt the danger from being witnesses in this case, but I liked to think it made our bond, as the guys called it, stronger.

My father was, of course, convicted. Why he thought he'd get away with his stuff was ridiculous, but that's the arrogance of criminals. Just because you have an expensive lawyer doesn't mean that you'll get off. This one time, the state had an air-tight case.

With the testimony of Zain, Marcus, Drew, Cole, and myself, my father got the book thrown at him. Conspiracy to commit murder against a Federal agent made it quite literally a federal case and sentencing on that can go any number of years to life. My father got thirty years on that charge and another ten for kidnapping me. If he ever got out, he'd be a very old man.

But that wasn't the end of it. A couple of his crew didn't relish spending the rest of their lives behind bars and opted for lives as Witsec witnesses and spilled their guts to the authorities. They helped to build cases against other Satan Son's divisions, and the club became a shadow of itself.

Zain and I returned from the last of the trials where we had to testify. He was driving because you can't get the steering wheel away from that man. He seemed glum, however, and didn't seem to want to talk.

I learned it never did any good to ask him what was wrong. You just need to start talking to draw him out.

"I'm glad it's over," I said.

"Yeah," he said.

"We can start a new part of our lives."

Normally quiet Zain communicated even less. I didn't know what was bothering him. I couldn't dig a single response out of him, and we were running out of time because we turned up the private road that led to the lodge.

"Zain?"

He harrumphed.

"You can do anything you want now and don't need us to protect you."

I froze. What was he trying to tell me? Did the guys not want me around anymore?"

"Well, that's true. What's going on, Zain?"

"You'll see," he said.

Zain had that 'I'm not talking about this,' tone in his voice which I had found was reserved for discussions with the group.

No one said a poly-relationship was easy.

He parked the truck and when I got out, he nodded his head toward the beach.

"Let's go there."

"Why?" I said slowly.

"Please. We have things to discuss."

I was freaking out because I'd never seen Zain so serious. My heart pounded in my chest. They really don't want me to stay anymore. I knew it. Despite the good times, the past year hadn't been easy. Though the guys loved each other like brothers, there was some sibling rivalry too, and a lot of it centered on who got to spend what time when with me. But I thought we'd worked that out.

Marcus, Drew, and Cole stood on the beach with their hands clasped in front of them, and I gulped. I almost felt like I was on one of those "reality" bachelorette shows, but instead of me handing roses to certain guys, it looked like they formed a rebellion and were kicking me out of the house.

Zain went and stood in line with them. The sun was beginning to set and spread a rosy glow on the water. It would be peaceful except for the four very grim men in front of me.

"Hey, guys. What's up? Zain says we need to talk?"

"Well," said Marcus. "We're wondering what your plans are."

"Yeah," said Drew. "For the rest of your life."

"Zain said that I don't need you anymore."

"All the trials are done. Your father and much of his club are in jail. You'd probably be safe enough if you wanted to leave."

"It's not like we gave you much of chance with this mate thing," said Cole.

"Have any of you changed how you feel?"

Marcus shook his head. "No, Ellie. But we know we've been a little much sometimes, and we just want you to be happy."

"But I am happy."

"See, I told you," said Cole.

"We've.." said Marcus, "We've been talking about this, and human customs don't fit this situation, but we think—"

"Oh, get to it," said Cole. I smiled. He was the most spontaneous but also the most impatient.

"You are our mate always," said Drew.

"But we are wondering if you want a more formal arrangement," said Zain.

"I don't understand."

"Marry us," spurted out Cole.

"Or rather," said Marcus, "we'd all say the words, but legally you'd marry Zain."

"This is what you want to talk to me about?" I started laughing.

"What's so funny?" demanded Zain.

"I'm not going to do that."

"See," said Drew hitting Cole's arm. "I told you. She doesn't want to stay with us."

"No. I didn't mean that either. I love you, all of you, and I don't need a wedding ceremony to memorialize that. As far as I'm concerned, you're my mates and my husbands, and that's that.

"See," said Zain smiling with satisfaction. "I told you all."

I'd been thinking about this for a while, and I didn't know how they'd feel but it was time to spring this on them.

"I haven't changed my name legally yet. How about instead of Ellie Walters, I take the name Ellie Clark? That way we all have the same name. How does that sound?"

"What do you say, guys? Should Ellie become a Clark?"

"Hell yeah!" exclaimed Cole, and before I knew it, all four men surrounded me in one great hug.

EPILOGUE - ELLIE

After everything that happened these past few days, we decided to go back to the lodge but I had to admit, rest and relaxation were the furthest things from my mind.

I never thought I'd find one guy to share my life with, never mind four and now that I'd found them, I definitely wanted to show my appreciation.

We'd barely made it into the living room before Zain pushed my hair off my shoulders and planted tender kisses from the nape of my neck to my ear. His voice was husky and his breath was hot when he whispered, "Always be ours, Ellie and we'll always be yours." My insides melted at how sweet Zain, our Alpha could be.

I was also glad to know that my desire was matched by his.

A felt another warm body come up behind me and turned around to find Marcus there. I'm pressed between the two of them and it felt more right than anything I've ever done before. My softness against their hardness and the smell of men, *my* men!

Zain kissed me slowly at first, but his yearning soon turned to hunger; his tongue searched for mine. At the same time, Marcus's hands came up between us, cupping my breasts as he bit the skin on my neck, eliciting a moan.

Marcus slid his hands underneath my shirt, finding my nipples beneath my bra and using his thumbs, stroked them until they hardened. Another moan prompted his hands towards the front of my jeans, searching for the button standing in the way of our closeness.

Soon we are a tangle of naked limbs, touching, kissing and exploring.

I opened Zain's fly and slipped my hand inside, wrapping them around his growing length. His cock stiffened at my touch and seemed to grow larger with every stroke.

I slid down, wanting to give him a closer inspection but Zain came down with me, flipping me on to my back quickly before I can even utter a protest. "There'll be time for that later."

"I can't wait any longer to be inside you." He pulled his pants down and flung them aside in one quick motion.

"I don't want to wait either." I lowered my panties and spread my legs, hot with desire as he leaned over me. He lined himself up, the head of his staff grazing the entrance of my wetness.

He paused just as his thickness parted my waiting lips. My need was palpable. "I want you inside me now."

He slid in, slowly inch by inch, filling me up. His gentleness was sweet but it was also killing me. After the events of the past few days and the love I felt for him, Marcus, Drew and Cole, I knew I wanted him – I wanted all of them in a way I'd never wanted anyone or anything before.

I smiled at him and pressed my hips into his, urging him to continue.

He had a look of ecstasy on his face as he heeded my call; his thrusts soon became quicker, harder and more rhythmic.

He suddenly pulled out and turned me onto my side, spooning me. With his arm wrapped around me and our legs entwined, his cock again finds a rhythm.

"How's that feel baby?"

"Oh... it's so good," I manage to gasp out as his last thrust delved deliciously deep.

While Zain fucked me from behind, Marcus came in for a passionate kiss. He was fully naked now and I couldn't believe my luck. He turned his attention to my breasts, lavishing them with kisses and gentle nips. Then he reached down and found my clit with his thumb, rubbing it. That sensation combined with Zain's thrusts were almost too much for me.

"Oh fuck. I'm close! I'm..." Suddenly the overwhelming sensation takes over as waves of pleasure course through my body. I felt Zain's body tense as my clenching pushed him over the edge and he exploded. He kept thrusting, pumping his sweetness into me, and I wanted all of it.

As he pulled out, satiated, he gave me a lingering kiss that said everything would be ok as long as we were together.

Marcus took my hand and positioned me on top and I slid onto him, supporting my weight with my knees, taking it slowly now that part of my appetite had been filled. But when I started to pull back, he grabbed my hips and slammed me down onto him, filling me completely. He cock was thicker than Zain's but I was so wet by then, it felt so good, too good almost.

I looked over at Cole and Drew, inviting them over with a nod.

They approached together; their eyes full of hunger.

I reached for Cole's cock, that was already standing at

attention and stroked it a few times before I couldn't resist any longer. I wanted to feel his length in my mouth. I wanted to hear him moan for me.

I circled his tip with my tongue, teasing him as I flicked and sucked before I took what I could of his cock. He groaned with pleasure, which only egged me on more. My body couldn't quite process all of the pleasure coursing through me. I was still riding Marcus, who met my every downward motion with an equal thrust of his own.

Not wanting to be left out, Drew pressed up against my back with his hardness, reminding me that more was yet to come. He kissed my neck and licked the length of my back, sending shivers up my spine. I looked back at him and saw him take his length in his hand. He started stroking himself, getting himself ready for me.

My bouncing was starting to take a toll on Marcus, and his thrusts became shorter and more frantic as he pushed me down harder and harder.

"Marcus, if you keep that up, I'm going to come!"

"Come for me, come for me as I fuck you."

As he said that, my pleasure exploded for the second time and Cole came as well; the sight of me coming was too much for him.

I was tired but I still no less excited and I wanted Drew. He'd been so loving and so patient throughout everything. There was no way he'd get less than my undivided attention.

"Are you ok?" He asked.

"I will be once I've had you," I replied.

He smiled back at me and spun me around in response, positioning my ass in the air and quickly slid himself inside in one quick motion. I couldn't get over how different each of them felt and how their immense love for me allowed us to share these moments together.

His cock slid in and out, stopping once every few strokes to stop and tease me before plunging in again with his full length, making me catch my breath. I was so sensitive by that point, every nerve on my body was tingling. I only hoped I made him feel just as good.

Suddenly, he slid out, released me and pushed me onto the ground.

He lifted my legs onto his shoulders and pulled me up towards him, sliding in at a new angle where I could feel his balls slap into me with every thrust. "I want to look into your eyes as I come inside you." I reached down to fondle him as he motions became frenzied. With a grunt, I could feel him release but he kept going.

"I'm not going to stop until you come for me too."

As I felt him fill me up, his hot seed pushed me over the edge and I cried out, "Oh god, I'm coming with you," as he collapsed on top of me.

I was happier than I'd ever been and I knew that as Ellie Clark, my life was all my own. No one could take it away from me and that meant everything.

*Did you love **Mated to the Clan**? The next story is Courtney's in **Protected by the Pack**. Courtney leaves for Afghanistan, determined to prove her father wrong. But now, her life is in danger and she's surrounded by secrets; ones worth killing for. Can she trust these soldiers she hardly knows to keep her safe?*

books2read.com/protectedbythepack

Or continue reading for a sneak peek!

PROTECTED BY THE PACK

COURTNEY

I was frustrated as I sat at the little desk in the tent and typed out an email to my boss. I didn't want to quit...I'm really not a quitter, and besides, my father would kill me if I did. But I had just about as much of this as I could take and I expected my boss to do something about it...something like bringing me back home.

It was mostly my father's fault that I was in my current predicament, and as I typed, I thought about how his controlling nature had landed me here...as close to hell as I would probably ever get. It started way back when I graduated high school...or maybe even way back before that. Yes, it had actually started the day I was born. My father is a control freak. He's retired military, a Lieutenant General, and he doesn't know civilians don't take orders, especially if they're your family.

Behind his back I refer to him as "The General". The General was the one who had pressured me into picking a major when I first started college. I hadn't known what or who I wanted to be at that point in my life. I was barely eighteen years old, and had lived a sheltered life in Sherman

Oaks, a comfortable suburb of the San Fernando Valley in L.A. My mother and I kept each other company in the same house they'd bought when they first married, while my father traveled, sometimes for months or even years at a time. In other words, when he did come home, we barely knew each other. Yet somehow he still insisted on controlling my life.

The General had missed my high school graduation. He'd missed my first semester in college. But as my bad luck would have it, he decided it was time for retirement just as I was entering my second semester as a Liberal Arts major. When he arrived home and found out what my major was, I thought his head might explode. I tried to explain to him that it was only temporary until I grew to know myself better and knew exactly what I wanted to do with my life. The General's response to that, was that if I didn't figure out who I was and what I wanted by my second year in college, I would need to find myself a way to pay for my own education and living expenses. I was so pissed off by that, I almost took him up on it. My mother was the one that gave me a dose of reality. She told me that she'd met the General while she herself was working as a waitress and struggling to put herself through college. She told me about living in a run-down apartment, working twelve hours a day, attending school for six, and sleeping four hours, just to wake up and do it all over again the next day, wasn't a life. She admitted to having regrets about not following through with a career and instead, becoming a stay at home mother and military wife. But she had made me realize that six more years under my father's thumb might well be worth the alternative.

So, I did some soul searching and I'd decided that my curious mind coupled with my interest in reading and writing and my grasp of the English language, was a perfect fit for a journalism degree. My knack for foreign languages could come in handy too. For a while, I'd been happy with my choice. I loved the classes, excelled in them, and along the way I started picturing myself in the future, working for a television news show and traveling the world, reporting on things like politics and current events that were shaping the world. But after graduating UCLA with honors and going on to complete a Master's program, I was stunned to find out that no matter how good my grades were, or how well I had done in my internship program for a widely popular periodical in Los Angeles...getting a real job in the news industry was next to impossible. Our economy was in a slump, and the job market was completely saturated.

I spent the first whole year after college, applying and interviewing for jobs. I worked a string of low-paying jobs that I was ridiculously over qualified for, anything to keep from asking The General for help. I wasn't happy or fulfilled in my career, but I was doing it on my own. And as frustrating as it was to wake up every morning knowing that I would be doing nothing more important with my day than covering a dog and cat show or a chili cook-off or high school football game, it was still better than being dependent on my father. I dated occasionally, but out of fear of ending up like my mother someday, completely overshadowed by the man in my life, I avoided relationships.

The General was not happy with the choices I was making. He liked to remind me that I was only a few years away from being thirty with a dead-end job, no husband and no kids, like if those things never happened for me, my entire life would be insignificant. In hindsight, I wished that I would have cut him off completely...but I hadn't, and now here I was in a place I called hell, just because I'd been so determined to prove a point to a man that would never get me anyways.

I had just worked an eight hour day, reporting on a horticulture show...in the rain. I arrived home, wet, tired and frustrated to find The General waiting at my door. He had come bearing what he called 'a gift.' He had an old army buddy who was now the station manager for a small television station in Atlanta. He was willing to give me a job...supposedly, reporting on 'real news.' I was skeptical, but I was a big believer of trying to see the positive in negative situations. The first and most important positive was that I would be 3000 miles away from my retired and intrusive father. The second, it couldn't be any worse than the job I was doing now, and it paid almost twice as much.

So, less than a month after my father made the call to his friend in Atlanta, I packed up my studio apartment and boarded a plane from LAX to Atlanta. I checked into the hotel I would be staying at until I found an apartment on Saturday. Bright and early Monday morning, I reported to work. I felt like my excitement was almost palpable to everyone in the building that morning, and by late afternoon, so was my disappointment.

The station manager assigned me to "assist" a middle-aged anchor named Lana right off the bat. Lana had big, blonde, heavily hair sprayed hair and a plastic face. She was as thin as a rail and her skin looked like it hadn't seen the sun in years. On air, the smile on her face was plastered almost as tightly as her hair, but off, she was demanding, irritable and from what I could determine, miserable with her own life. She seemed to take that out on those closest to her and I quickly became one of her scapegoats. Reminding myself daily that this job was an opportunity and I wouldn't be Lana's assistant forever, I grinned and bore it for months. After six of those harrowing months had passed, I thought my big break had finally arrived.

I arrived one morning to a message that the station manager wanted to see me right away. His words to me were,

"I have an assignment overseas and I need someone who doesn't have too many commitments here in the states to take it. I don't know how long you'll be there."

"Where is 'there' exactly?"

"Afghanistan, near Kabul."

I felt my heart begin to race. I wasn't sure if it was the excitement of the prospect of this assignment...or fear of the unknown. But what I did know was that it was the first time in months that I had really felt alive. Without asking too many questions, which in hindsight I regretted, I took it. What I knew when I got on the plane to Kabul, was that I would be stationed at a military base where a team of doctors from the US ran a medical clinic. Their time there was all voluntary, and self-financed, along with donations from generous benefactors in the states. The station wanted an in-depth story, a documentary...and if I did a good job, my name on the credits of that documentary could very well shoot my career to the top of that pyramid I had been struggling so hard to climb.

Hindsight...sometimes was a bitch. I didn't ask any questions about what life would be like on the base. My father never talked about his time in the army and I had never been interested enough to ask. The first few weeks I was there, was like culture shock. and I tried listing out the positives in my head every day. But as the days went by, that was getting harder. I had started out with a pretty good list. My travel was funded, I got a clothing allowance, and I was surrounded by hot, muscular men. Of course the travel was to the middle of the desert. It was hot, dry and buggy. The clothes I spent the allowance on were baggy khaki pants, camouflage vests, hiking boots and a hijab I had to wear if I went off base, which was rare. The men were plentiful, but they were quiet, serious and heavily armed. And the doctors I was there to do a story about were oddly tight-lipped and unwelcoming. My cameraman was a retired veteran who smoked too much and drank whiskey straight out of the bottle all day. My meals were served in packages. They were called 'MRE's' and rarely resembled the description on the label. I wanted to go home...and after three weeks of struggling with both my conscience and the idea of facing my father as being a "quitter" I was finally composing the email that I hoped would put an end to my misery.

I stopped to wipe the sweat out of my eyes for at least the dozenth time since I sat down in front of the laptop. It was hot...not, *'California in the summer'* hot, but *'this is hell'* hot. At least I didn't have to wear the hijab while I was on base. It seemed to trap all that heat in my body and I couldn't help but wonder how the Afghani women didn't melt from the inside out. As it were, I couldn't find a deodorant strong enough to make me feel fresh for more than five minutes and that was even pressing it. My lips were dry and chapped and my skin flaked off thanks to the ever-present wind. Everything was perpetually covered in dust. When I looked out beyond the gates of the small base all I saw was dust - piles of it, everywhere. It was like being on a deserted island, without the trees or the ocean.

Daytime was bad enough, but night was the worst. As I lay in my tent and tried to sleep, there were constant sounds off in the distance of guns or bombs going off. That troubled me, especially since I'd been assured before I left the states that American's were simply still there to 'keep' the peace. So far however I'd seen no signs of that peace. The base was constantly locked down and they had drills almost daily to prepare us for the possibility of a terrorist attack. But what troubled me most of all at night were the howls. I could hear wolves, so many of them, howling and whining all night long. They sounded close, too close to be outside the gates. But when I asked anyone else about them in the light of day, they all denied they even heard them. At times I felt like I might be losing my mind. And it was after one such restless night that I decided I just couldn't do this any longer. I had to go home.

I was just about to type about the wolves in my email when suddenly one of the soldiers stuck his head inside the tent. I didn't recognize this one...I would have remembered him. He was big, and although he was buried in army gear, I could almost imagine what his body might look like without it. Of course I'd been without manly company for quite some time now. Atlanta hadn't offered much in the way of a dating pool while I was there,, and then there was the three weeks in hell. He was incredibly hot though. Even his eyes were captivating. They were green, but with a ring around the irises that was a dark amber color, unlike anything I'd ever seen. I was lost in them for a few seconds, strangely so...looking into his eyes gave me the strangest feeling of warmth, and peace. until I snapped out of it, and finally processed what he was saying.

"We have to go."

"Excuse me? Go where? We weren't scheduled to go anywhere according to my briefing this morning."

The civilians, myself and the five doctors, were given a briefing every morning. We were told how many refugees would be brought out to the clinic for treatment, or if we'd be allowed to go into town for supplies...or sometimes if the base would be locked down that day. When that was the case we never received an explanation.

"Now. We have to go now."

Something in his eyes told me this was no ordinary trip into town. "Are we coming back?"

"I don't have time for questions. Come on, let's go."

"What about my stuff?"

"Leave it, we don't have time."

"Can I bring my laptop?" When I first arrived, I was told there might be the possibility of evacuation drills or even an emergency evacuation. This might be a drill, or it might be a real evacuation. Either way, no matter how boring the story I'd done so far, I wasn't leaving it behind.

"If you grab it and come now." I was looking around the tent. I hadn't brought much with me, but if we weren't coming back, I hated leaving it there. It would only take seconds for me to pack it all in the big canvas bag that I'd brought. "Hurry," he barked at me. I glared at him, and moved slower.

$\mathcal{I}$ was a Green Beret and I didn't have the patience to handle anyone, especially some princess reporter, with kid gloves. That's why I had taken a post outside the base for the past month. That, and the fact that I wasn't sure I'd even be able to control myself that close to a woman. The team had been assigned to "watch over" the military base and the six civilians currently bunking there. At first it seemed like an odd assignment. We weren't normally assigned to babysit anyone, especially civilians. The civilian men were doctors, a medical team who had come to Kabul to start a free clinic for the refugees. They'd been allowed to do that on base for their safety, and the safety of the people they'd be treating. But the soldiers stationed there should have been protection enough. A team of Green Berets was overkill, in my mind.

Then a week after the doctors showed up, the reporter arrived. I had been told she was coming and their orders were to make sure she stayed on base and none of them were to touch her. That was like putting a candy bar in front of a five-year-old and telling him he couldn't eat it. The only women my team had seen in the past two years had been those dressed in traditional Afghani garb, covered from head to toe with only a pair of eyes showing. Those pretty brown eyes had even become tempting after a while, but my team and I had orders not to touch any of them, and we were all good little soldiers.

I spent many nights once the reporter arrived however, tossing and turning in my tent. The descriptions of her alone that the men had given me were enough to drive me crazy at this point. But there was also her scent. Even from three hundred yards away I could smell her, and sight unseen, I wanted her. And then I stuck my head in that tent and realized that my team's descriptions hadn't done her justice. If I had met her in a bar, at least a year and a half ago, I would have had one goal in mind, and that would be getting those baggy, khaki pants off of her. I felt a stirring in my loins just thinking about it. It had been way too long since I'd been allowed to spend any time with a woman. Way too long.

The reporter's khaki pants and green t-shirt wasn't the sexiest outfit I'd ever seen by a long-shot, but it was definitely the sexiest I'd seen in this Godforsaken desert. I could at least see that she had a waistline, and a pair of breasts that I would like to see more of. She was about five-five or six and she looked fit, like she worked out. Her hair was dark blonde, wild and curly. It had that untamed look to it that made a man, especially an extremely horny man, think about wrapping his hands up in it. Her eyes were light blue, almost clear, and when she turned to look at me, it felt for a second like she was looking right through me. I was suddenly worried that she could see who and what I really was.

I was a 'normal' man when I joined the army right out of high school. I had always been athletic and adventurous, and I was in good physical shape when I joined. After boot camp I was even stronger and more fit. I spent some time in

Australia and Germany, which were pretty tame posts, but we still drilled every day and I kept getting stronger. The great part about the 'tame' posts was that I got to spend my time off in town, going to bars and clubs with my friends,, and getting into a lot of foreign ladies' panties. But even that got boring after a while. The war was over and the only teams still seeing any action were the Special Forces. So when the opportunity arose to try out for the Green Berets, I couldn't pass it up. I was 23 years old then, and I'd been a Green Beret for five years. I was trained in unconventional warfare, foreign internal defense, special reconnaissance, direct action and counter terrorism. I'd been involved in combat search and rescue missions, counter narcotics missions, counter proliferation and hostage rescue. And then one night in the midst of what the army called a 'humanitarian assistance' mission, everything changed. I hated my life now, most especially the cursed instinct to survive that kept me and every man on my team from ending it. I brought myself out of my thoughts and back to the assignment at hand. The reporter was dragging her feet, and we needed to move.

"Move! Now!" I yelled at her.

Her body jerked like I startled her and the glare she sent shooting in my direction darkened and deepened. Somehow as much as I was annoyed, the fact that she recovered so quickly impressed me.

"Don't yell at me. I'm not under your command. I'm taking my stuff..."

I was impressed with her moxy, but we had to get out of there, and I was done playing. I took two steps into the tent, grabbed the reporter around her small waist, lifted her up off the ground and threw her over my shoulder. She screamed and kicked while cussing me out in colorfully educated language, but I ignored her. Everyone was busy, moving what they needed from the base into the trucks, so no one paid much attention to us as I carried her across the dirt lot and to the waiting truck. I dumped her into the back where the five doctors already sat and as soon as I let go of her, she tried to come at me like a wild banshee with her claws out. I didn't normally show my wolf in the daylight, or to humans, but I really didn't have time for this one. I lifted one corner of my mouth and let my canines drop and I knew without being able to see them that my eyes were glowing. She let out a loud gasp and stumbled backward into the truck, right before I slammed the door and pounded my palm against the back of it, to let the driver know we were locked and loaded.

I double checked that everyone else was off base and then I climbed into the passenger seat of the Hummer we'd be chasing the truck carrying the civilian's. There was a Jeep in front of that truck. Everyone else on base, all Army personnel, were loaded into another big truck and already headed toward the next rendezvous spot. My team, for the first time since we'd started working together, was not following orders. We were taking these people in the opposite direction. We were getting the civilians out of Afghanistan and sealing our own teams fate in the process.

"We're good to go, brother," I said to the driver, Will Blunt, another Green Beret and one of my teammates for the full five years I'd been a part of the Special Forces.

"That reporter gave you a bit of trouble I see?" Will chuckled and put the Hummer in gear, pulling out of the gates onto the dirt road behind the truck.

I sighed and said, "I showed her my canines."

Will hit the brakes.

"What the hell? Clayton, you know how dangerous that can be."

"Speaking of dangerous, the truck is getting too far ahead of us. Will accelerated and dust began to billow behind us as we caught up to the truck. The dust between us was so thick that it was like fog, but we were used to it. Thank God for wide open spaces and good eyesight.

"What were you thinking?"

"I wasn't. She just pissed me off. She was acting like a princess...like she thought the moving van was coming for her stuff and the limousine to take her to the airport."

Will chuckled again. "I'll bet the back end of that truck is 115 degrees. Probably unlike any limousine she's ever ridden in."

"Good. Maybe by the time we get her to the airport and on a plane, any romantic notions she had about visiting the Middle East will be out of her head. Women like her don't belong in places like this."

Will cocked an eyebrow. "Women like her?"

"You know, pretty, soft..." I felt that stirring again. "Spoiled American women. She should be home making sandwiches and having babies."

Will threw his head back and laughed.

"Boy, it's a good thing I'm the only one here to hear you say that. Women would chew you up and spit you out for talking like that, especially if you did it stateside where they pride themselves on being able to do everything men can do." God how I wished for just an hour with one who wanted to do what only a woman could do. I chuckled along with Will, but there was nothing happy about it. I needed a woman, but even more than that, I wanted to go home.

The mention of 'stateside' made me sad. I missed my family -my parents, sister and my niece and two nephews. I missed my hometown and the friends I'd had for as long as I could remember. I swallowed the lump in my throat and tried to push those thoughts away I said, "Whatever. You and I both know they're not made to withstand what we do out here. It's why none of us will ever have a mate. No way even after..." Will frowned. "Sorry buddy, I know you hate to hear that." All Will had ever wanted was to fall in love, get married and have half a dozen kids once he finished his tour. Now it looked like casual sex and one-night-stands was what we were all destined for. I wasn't happy with having to wait for that even, but I had no problem with the idea of not having a mate. The thought of being with one woman forever practically made my skin crawl. I'd been told that wolves mate for life, but the human part of me wasn't on board with that, even if it was a possibility out here, which I doubted.

The '5' of us had been a team for five years before all the shit happened, and another year and a half since the night that changed us all forever. Not a day went by since then that at least one of us didn't wish, out loud, that we'd been left up there to die. I thought it myself on a regular basis, because now, even dying would be a long shot.

Luke 'Titan' Bloomfield slid open the back of the truck. Luke was another one of my teammates, and best friends. We called him Titan, because he was six-foot-six, three-hundred plus pounds and his body looked like it was made out of steel. Luke was the kind of guy that would send people to walk on the other side of the street to keep from passing him too closely. He kept his black hair so short that that what was left was more like stubble than hair. His black beard was quite often grown out almost to the center of his chest and he had gray eyes that were so dark they looked black pits of tar. The ironic thing about Titan was that of the five of us, he was the nicest and the most sensitive if you gave him a chance. Even animals didn't fear him, unless he was in the mood to show them his fangs.

I shifted my focus to the inside of the truck once the door

was rolled up. The six people inside looked tired, hot, and frightened. Well, five of them looked frightened. The only female, the little blonde, spit-fire reporter, just looked pissed. In her defense, they had all been crammed into a truck that was already full of military equipment. We'd gotten the call to move and to pack everything we could into the truck. The civilians had been sitting on top of tents and sleeping bags with their backs up against the walls that were filled with communications equipment, guns and other paraphernalia. But in my defense, if the woman hadn't been such a pain in the ass in the first place, I had planned on letting her ride in the Hummer with me and Will.

"Where are we?" She was the first one to speak, of course, and it was in a demanding tone that irritated me all over again. I ignored her and instead looked at the doctor who sat covered in sweat and waiting patiently to be told what was going on.

"Dr. Steinbeck, you and your team can step out first, please."

"Excuse me!" I was beginning to envision the reporter with a gag in her mouth. Unfortunately that turned me on a little bit, so I had to put that thought out of my mind as well. Ignoring her again, I reached up to help the doctor step down off the back of the truck. One at a time, five men, stepped down off the truck. Manny, team member number four was already leading the five of them toward our other teammate, and the spot where they would soon be loaded onto an airplane and taken out of here.

"You can get out now," I told the reporter.

"No." She folded her arms and sat back against the wall of the truck. I rolled my eyes. I wondered if she was married or had a boyfriend. In other words, I wondered who I should feel sorry for.

"No?"

"No. I'm not getting out until you tell me where we are and what we're doing here."

"We're in Afghanistan. The exact location is classified, but we're at an airstrip where we'll be putting you on a plane and sending you home."

"Home?"

"Yes. Home." Suddenly it was like a light had been turned on inside of her. She had been hot before when she was sullen and angry. Now, she was purely beautiful, and for a second I forgot that I didn't like her. I stared at her until the look in her eyes changed slightly, almost like she recognized the lust in mine. Then it changed again, like she was remembering something. "Your eyes...they changed color earlier, and your teeth..."

"Come on or you're going to miss your plane." She had that suspicious, curious look that I had seen on the faces of journalists before, but it was obvious that she wanted to get home. She sighed and still clutching that laptop to her chest, stepped out of the truck and looked around. We were at a deserted airstrip in the middle of nowhere. There was one old hangar that looked like it had been built 80 years ago and never upgraded, a landing strip and a tower. That was the extent of it. No one had manned the tower in years. The airstrip was badly in need of repairs as well, every few feet there was a crack or a pothole. I could see her taking it all in, and then she frowned and said,

"Where's the plane?" As if on cue, we heard the sound of the twin-engine, six-seat Cessna 206 coming in from the west over the mountaintop. She frowned again when she saw it. "We're not flying all the way home in that, are we?"

I chuckled and almost told her they were, just to piss her off again. At the last minute however I said, "No. They'll fly you into Jalalabad and from there..."

"Jalala what?"

"It's a city in Nangarhar." She shrugged and it was my turn to frown. "It's a province of Afghanistan. Didn't do too well in geography class, I'm guessing?"

"Must you be an ass?"

"You bring it out in me," I said with a smile. She sighed and headed toward where the rest of the civilians were waiting. Manny, Will and Titan were in position to wave the plane in. Mitchell, who had driven the tank that led our little convoy, was in place to keep the civilians back, away from the small airstrip until the plane landed and they were ready to board. My eyes moved to the sexy sway of the reporter's hips as she walked toward the others. *Damn,* she was the finest thing I'd seen in a long time. I was thinking now that it was too bad that I hadn't taken security detail on her before the evacuation. My eyes were still on those sexy hips and my mind completely in the gutter when the explosion threw me to the ground, the plane circled around and left. Just like that, our plans were shot to hell - again.

books2read.com/protectedbythepack

Warlock's Claim

Historical Paranormal Romance

Secrets of Storyville

A Countess Betrayed

A Harlot Betrothed

Epic World Building Academy Romance

The Broken Academy

Power of Fire

Power of Magic

Power of Blood

Pacts & Promises

Bonds

Reverse Harem Escapes – Great for a Quick Roll in the Hay with None of the Guilt

Fated Shifter Mates

Mated to the Pack

Mated to Team Shadow

Mated to the Pride

Taming Her Bears

Mated to the Clan

Protected by the Pack

Claimed by the Pack

The Descendants :

Desired by Four

Fate of Three

Shared by the Four

Mates & Magic

The Sharing Spell

The Spell's Price

Backfired Magic